JOURNEY TO **STAR WARS: THE LAST JEDI**

STAR WARS™

THE LEGENDS OF
LUKE SKYWALKER

KEN LIU

ILLUSTRATED BY J. G. JONES

Disney • LUCASFILM

PRESS

LOS ANGELES • NEW YORK

For Esther and Miranda.
May the Force be with you, always.
—K. L.

For Dawn, thank you for all your care,
love and patience. You are my Force.
—J. G. J.

For information address Disney • Lucasfilm Press,
1101 Flower Street, Glendale, California 91201.
Printed in the United States of America
First Hardcover Edition, October 2017
3 5 7 9 10 8 6 4 2
FAC-008598-17338
ISBN 978-1-4847-8077-0
Designed by Leigh Zieske
Library of Congress Control Number on file
Visit the official *Star Wars* website at: www.starwars.com.

SUSTAINABLE FORESTRY INITIATIVE Certified Sourcing www.sfiprogram.org SFI-00993
Logo Applies to Text Stock Only

LUKE SKYWALKER?

I THOUGHT HE WAS A MYTH.

—REY

THE *WAYWARD CURRENT*

THE LONG-HAUL TRANSPORT BARGE *Wayward Current* was almost through its six-week journey from the wild, sparsely populated Mooshie Cluster to glitzy, flamboyant Canto Bight on the planet Cantonica. The deckhands gathered on the mess deck had just come off their watch; they were there to eat, socialize, and play games before catching a few hours of sleep.

They made a motley crew—some humanoid and human, a few reptilian and avian, and even a few droids. Almost all the deckhands were still short of full maturity by the standards of whatever species they belonged to. That was important, because Tuuma the Hutt, captain of the *Wayward Current*, insisted on having a crew the majority of which were still so enchanted by the boundless possibilities of the future that they would accept next to no pay in exchange for a chance to see the galaxy.

Ulina, the third mate, drained her pungent, tongue-burning Olo tea as a loud moan echoed through the dimly lit corridors of the barge, like the last dregs of steam departing from the furnace of an old moisture farm. She scanned through the dozen or so deckhands gathered around the low rusty table, wolfing down their food, and settled on a lanky fifteen-year-old girl with cropped hair.

"Sounds like the feisty filly in the corner stall is having trouble sleeping." The patch over Ulina's left eye glowed red with annoyance. "Did you do the endurance exercises with her in the double-gravity chamber today? You know fathiers need heavy exercise when they're cooped up on a ship like this."

"Sorry," said Teal, the fifteen-year-old. "I had to clean the reflux combusters—"

"No excuses," said Ulina. "Each of these fathiers is worth more than three years of your wages. Go fix your mistake."

"Do I get only half rations next meal?" asked Teal timidly.

"You've been making a lot of mistakes on this trip. Almost late for some chore every day." Though her tone was severe, the red glow in Ulina's eye patch faded to a gentler orange. "But . . . we've been shorthanded. If you finish and come back quickly, I might not even remember that you had to do your chores out of order. I'm old, as some of you keep reminding me."

The young deckhands around the table chuckled at this. No one knew where Ulina was from, but it was said that she was older than all the deckhands put together. The gruff third mate had a kind streak in her that was all too rare among the desperadoes who plied the long-haul trade routes to eke out a living.

"If you dawdle and the first mate runs into you when

he makes his rounds, though, you'll have to go hungry. He's got a much better memory than I."

Chastened but also relieved, Teal stuffed her bread and nutrient paste tube into her pockets as she got up from the table.

"You're acting like we're going to steal your food," said G'kolu, a twelve-year-old Anlari boy whose fleshy horns were only as long as a human finger. The horns curled to show his amusement. "You're not going to enjoy eating that in the stinking fathier stalls anyway. Leave it here. I promise it will be here when you get back."

"That's not why—" Teal stopped.

"What, are you planning on sharing it with the fathiers?" asked Jane, a girl from Tanto Winn, where everyone had green eyes. "That bit of bread isn't even enough to fill the gap between their teeth. They won't appreciate it."

Teal shook her head. "None of your business." She turned and ran off.

The echoes of her footsteps bounced against the bulkheads and partitions, drawing more groans and neighs from other fathiers, massive towering creatures of incredible speed and grace—when not confined in the cramped quarters of a spaceship. They stamped their four legs, each as big around as a tree trunk and a few meters tall, and the din they made took a while to subside.

G'kolu's horns twisted pensively, but he said nothing. The first rule of being on a deep-space crew was that you respected the privacy of others. Everyone had secrets.

Ulina turned to the rest of the deckhands. "Better get some sleep. We'll be in port by morning watch, and it's going to be a long day of unloading in Canto Bight."

"I'm thinking we need another serving of vegicus tails," said G'kolu. "Even the captain has to agree that we need energy to do the work, right?" The boy could wheedle for more food better than anyone else on the crew.

Ulina was about to object, but Dwoogan, the ship's cook, was already firing up the fryer on the other side of the counter. Dwoogan was a tall muscular woman whose scarred face hinted at a mysterious past. Somehow she always managed to turn the most revolting ingredients into something delicious—even the vegicus, the vermin that lived in the bilges and storage nooks of long-haul spaceships. On long voyages with limited supplies, a resourceful cook like Dwoogan sometimes turned to them as extra protein supplements.

Ulina grunted noncommittally, but the young deckhands could tell by the pulsing green glow of her eye patch that she had assented.

A tantalizing oily aroma soon filled the mess deck.

The deckhands let out a loud cheer that set off more groans from the fathiers in their pens in the ship's bowels.

"I wonder if we'll see anyone famous in Canto Bight," said G'kolu, his horns standing up eagerly. The city's immense fathier racetracks and crowded casinos were legendary.

"Who do you want to see?" asked Dwoogan. She dropped handfuls of vegicus tails into the boiling oil, making everyone's mouths water as the greasy scent filled their noses.

"The jockeys!" said Jane, her green eyes wide, as if she were already in the grandstands.

"The holo stars!" said G'kolu.

"The people who have so much money that they wear their clothes only once before throwing them away," said Tyra, a thirteen-year-old human girl whose family had scavenged in junkyards all over the galaxy.

"The heroes of the New Republic!" said Naldy, a

skinny boy with striped skin who wouldn't tell anyone where he was from.

"Any heroes in particular?" asked Dwoogan. Her tone was affectionate, playful. She stirred the tails with a ladle and didn't flinch as drops of hot oil splashed against her powerful arms.

"Luke Skywalker," said Naldy.

"But he hasn't been seen in years," said G'kolu, his horns making a skeptical half turn.

"Doesn't mean that he *wouldn't* be in Canto Bight," said Naldy defensively. "He rode tauntauns, didn't he? I bet he would make an amazing jockey."

"I bet he'd rather be in the piloting races," said G'kolu. "Way more money in those. I heard that he once made the Kessel Run in under twelve parsecs."

"You're thinking of someone else," said Tyra. She and G'kolu shared the same quarters and bickered like siblings. "Skywalker was the one who once took down twenty AT-ATs with his lightsaber."

The other young deckhands chimed in.

"My mother told me it was two hundred! And he rode a tauntaun while doing it."

"Tauntauns are even harder to ride than fathiers—"

"My uncle said he used magic to smash two Star Destroyers together—"

"It wasn't magic. It was just good piloting. And it was *six* Star Destroyers—"

"*Twee-BOOP eek eek eek—*"

"That's a name I haven't heard in a while," said Ulina. The children and droids instantly quieted. Ulina's eye patch pulsed from amber to magenta. "There are lots of stories about Luke Skywalker. Some of them might even be true."

The deckhands hung on every word. Ulina had seen far more of the galaxy than the rest of them, and there seemed to be nothing she didn't know.

"Tell us one?" pleaded G'kolu, his horns leaning forward eagerly.

"It's late," said Ulina.

The deckhands would not accept this.

"Just one! Please?"

"We'll work extra hard tomorrow."

"*Dwee BOOP tweetweetwee?*" Even the ship's ancient droid custodian, G2-X, joined the chorus as he set the platter of fried vegicus tails on the table.

Dwoogan came over and stood at the edge of the group, her arms crossed in front of her, a grin on her face.

Ulina looked at her. "What are you so pleased about?"

"Every night, you say no. And they manage to drag a story out of you anyway."

"Since you're mocking my ability to maintain discipline, I'm going to assign *you* the task of telling the story tonight." Ulina strained to keep the smile off her face but was not having an easy time of it.

The deckhands cheered again as they reached grubby

fingers for the platter of hot vegicus tails. A story from Dwoogan was an even better treat.

"All right. As it happens, I did once hear a story about Luke Skywalker. . . ."

I'M OUT OF IT FOR A LITTLE WHILE, AND EVERYONE GETS DELUSIONS OF GRANDEUR!

—HAN SOLO

THE MYTH BUSTER

I DIDN'T START MY LIFE AS A COOK, but you've probably guessed that already from these scars on my face. There was a time when I could make the Kessel Run in less than fifteen parsecs and piloted my own blockade skipper against the Trade Federation—but those are stories for another evening.

One day, after a particularly unpleasant bit of cat and mouse with two Imperial customs patrols, I stopped in Xu'hu for a bit of much-needed R & R. I landed on the shore of Vette Lake and made my way to the Dande Donjon, by reputation a welcoming watering hole for

THE LEGENDS OF LUKE SKYWALKER

anyone who wanted to play games of chance, drink well-brewed spice tea, swap tales with strangers who didn't probe into your past, and most important of all, pay in untraceable credits.

A group of disreputable-looking characters sat on a circle of benches by the spice tea bar.

"Double shot, light spice, don't hold back on the bubbles," a woman shouted to the droid bartender. She was dressed in an engineer's overalls, and the lines on her leathery face spoke of long years spent struggling to get obstinate machines to obey. After a second, she added, "And add all the blue milk powder you can dissolve in it."

The droid beeped in acknowledgment and began to prepare the sweet foamy concoction. Even I smacked my lips in anticipation.

Though I had never been to the Donjon before, I knew right away that this was the right crowd for me. There are as many types of drinking establishments as there are sentient species in the galaxy. In some places, customers could duel with blasters without anyone batting an eye. I, on the other hand, desired the company of people who preferred blue milk to mindspice.

"I'll have the same," I called out.

A few in the crowd glanced up at me and nodded in acknowledgment. A Togruta sitting with his back to me grunted and shifted on his bench, making room. I envied his ability to use his hornlike montrals to sense my presence.

The droid bartender brought my beverage over after a minute. I breathed in the luscious, tangy aroma and took a tentative sip, savoring the delightful sensation of tiny bubbles of sugary air bursting on my tongue. *Pure bliss.*

Only then did I begin to pay attention to the chatter around me. The engineer whose drink order I had copied was arguing a theory.

"I'm telling you, no one, and I mean *no one*, has ever

seen him eat anything, not even a dried Naboo sardine or a ration cracker." Her animated gestures and passionate voice held the crowd's rapt attention.

"But, Redy," my Togruta seatmate objected, "maybe he eats only when he's underwater."

"No," said the woman. "There are plenty of holos and pictures of rebels training underwater, and lots of them feature soldiers chomping down on good chow. That's basic propaganda one-oh-one, right? You want people to fight for you, you have to promise they'll at least get to eat. And you never see Ackbar eat anything in those, either."

"So what does that mean?" asked a man who wore a cowl that hid his face in shadow. A glass of blue milk stood in front of him—a traditional, wholesome choice. His voice was gravelly and deep, and in the flickering light from the Donjon's hovering firefly lamps, I could see he had a graying beard.

"So you have to put it all together," said Redy, a sly

and triumphant smile on her face. She leaned in to the circle of benches and lowered her voice conspiratorially. We all leaned in, too, as she counted off her points on her fingers, one by one.

"Think about it: his lip movements don't match his words exactly—we engineers notice stuff like that; rumors are rampant that he sometimes sits still for hours when he thinks no one is around to see; he's never been away from some power source for more than a day; and he's never been caught on cam eating." She paused, and the crowd held its breath. "The conclusion is inescapable: He. Is. Not. Real."

"What?" My Togruta companion almost spat out his tea, a dark broth-like drink that smelled of spiced meat.

Redy was only too happy to explain. "My guess is that Ackbar is a mindless droid draped in Mon Calamari skin and remotely operated by Rebel Alliance and New Republic bigwigs. He's literally a puppet."

Everyone was stunned into silence. I had heard

plenty of outrageous ideas in cantinas around the galaxy, but this one ranked among the most . . . original. After a moment, I asked, "Why . . . why would the New Republic create a puppet admiral?"

"It's about appearances." Redy was prepared for my skepticism. "Ackbar is handsome, tall, impressive-looking, and the backstory they made up for him tugs at the heartstrings. Who doesn't sympathize with a scrappy common soldier who worked his way up the ranks and turned into a brilliant strategist? But do you really believe an aquatic soldier who had never even piloted an X-wing could mastermind the incredible victories at Endor and Jakku? However, it sure made a great morale booster to say that he did."

"So you think someone else came up with those plans?" another woman asked. I liked her boots. They were tipped with figures of Kowakian monkey-lizards, a fun touch.

"Without a doubt. My guess is that Mon Mothma,

Leia Organa, Jan Dodonna, and the rest of them had a whole group of strategists and thinkers in some windowless hideout working for them. Like most engineers, they do the hard work but get no credit. Many of them probably aren't the photogenic type, what with years of studying in dimly lit military archives and sitting in front of computers all day to run simulations. Maybe they look too bookish, too short, too small, too plain. . . . The politicians needed a handsome symbol to rally the troops, and so they created Ackbar, the puppet admiral." She swept her hand through the air dramatically. "Never underestimate the power of propaganda."

"That's quite a theory," said the man with the cowl. I could hear a trace of amusement in his voice. "For an unlicensed engineer, you sure know a lot about politics."

Redy bristled. "I wasn't always on the run, living on scraps from fixing smugglers' rust buckets, you know! I went to the University of Coruscant and once worked on the most advanced starships in the Imperial shipyards. I got to meet and greet real admirals, and even showed a couple of grand moffs around the shipyards. I know what I'm talking about."

The man held out his hands and dipped his head slightly. "I meant no offense. The galaxy is a large place, and it's always refreshing to hear new stories. Why don't you enlighten us more?"

"I just pay more attention to details," a mollified Redy said with pride. "They don't call me Redy the Myth Buster for nothing. I've discovered even more elaborate conspiracies that will make your head spin."

Instead of saying more, she drained the last of her tea, sighed wistfully, and set down the mug with finality. She took a credit chip out of a small breast pocket and glanced at the display with a worried frown. "Guess it's time to find more work," she muttered.

Even though I knew exactly what she was doing,

I couldn't help falling for it. "Wait," I said, "you can't leave us hanging like that. I'll buy you another drink. Tell the story."

"I don't know." Redy licked her lips. "It's about a legend of the Rebellion, Luke Skywalker. But it's a pretty long story, and I'm also hungry—"

"I'll buy you dinner," the hooded man said. He leaned forward in his seat, and the hood slipped back a bit, revealing a pair of sharp eyes and a lined face that somehow managed to retain a hint of boyish mischief. "This, I gotta hear."

Her ploy a success, Redy called out to the droid bartender, "A *triple* shot, extra bubbles, a heap of blue milk powder—and get me a plate of Naboo sardine fritters with lava sauce. These two are paying!"

She leaned back, satisfied, and began her tale.

Everyone knows the officially sanctioned version of Luke Skywalker, last of the Jedi Knights, guardian of the galaxy, trusted operative of General Leia Organa, greatest pilot of the New Republic, mighty wielder of the emerald lightsaber, harbinger of victory in his X-wing with five red stripes. . . . I could go on and on.

Indeed, stories about him have spun so out of control that it's impossible to separate myth from facts. Well, that's where I come in.

Now, having had a good education and a career as a professional in the Empire, I know a bit more than the average smuggler about how political power works. It's all about theater and plots and backroom intrigue. You can't trust anything the talking holoheads on the newscasts tell you.

The truth is hidden out of sight, and you have to study a variety of sources and really use your brain to figure out what they don't want you to know.

Almost everything you think you know about Luke Skywalker is a lie.

Even his name was an invention. Orphaned as a child, back on Tatooine he was known as Luke Clodplodder. Brought up by his moisture-farming uncle and aunt, Luke grew into a lazy youth with severe delusions about his skills as a skyhopper pilot and mechanic—

"That's a bit harsh," muttered the hooded man. But Redy heard him.

"Not at all," she said. "I'll present you my evidence. Biggs Darklighter, who grew up with Clodplodder on Tatooine, was often cited as the source of Luke's exploits as a skyhopper pilot in Beggar's Canyon. But several Imperial Academy instructors have told me that Biggs was among the worst students they'd ever had at the academy, and his praise for young Clodplodder's piloting skills must be treated as the exaggerated tall tales of a similarly incompetent pilot."

"Tall tales, eh? You don't say," said the hooded man.

"I *do* say," said Redy, taking a big gulp of her extra-foamy drink and wiping her mouth with the back of her hand. "As for his skills as a mechanic, we know from multiple sources that he often went to Tosche Station on Tatooine for power converters—"

"Those things can be tricky—"

"Not unless the kid was lazy! Any real mechanic can tell you that power converters for moisture-farming equipment are designed to be rugged and easy to repair in the field. Buying new power converters once a year as they wear out may be excusable, but having to go multiple times a month meant that he was either incapable of fixing them or merely using them as an excuse to go to town to waste time with his similarly lazy friends."

The hooded man chuckled. "I guess I knew someone who would agree with you on that. Sorry to interrupt. Please continue."

Clodplodder might not have possessed any worthwhile skills to a civilized pair of eyes, but he did have two critical qualities that could be useful to an unscrupulous mind: he was good-looking and smooth talking.

After his uncle and aunt disappeared mysteriously, he left Tatooine. (My bet is that the uncle and aunt, like many poor farmers, could only make ends meet by dodging Imperial taxes. Eventually, the tax assessors hounding them became too much to bear, and they just packed up and skipped town. Lazy Luke probably got left behind because his relatives thought him a liability.)

The exact manner in which he left was never made clear in the official records, but by talking to many traders, fugitives, former Imperial troopers, and others who weren't paid or intimidated by the New Republic's propagandists, here's what I've been able to determine: Clodplodder joined a gang of criminals.

The head of the gang was Benny "Wiseman" O'Kenoby, an old con man who was the brains of the band. Other members included Hansel "Lightning Hands" Shooter, a seasoned Corellian smuggler and habitual liar who never kept a bargain, and Chewie "Shaggy" Baccarat, a Wookiee with a gambling addiction who served as the group's muscle and means of intimidation.

How did Luke "Babyface" Clodplodder fit in? He was the one who charmed the gang's victims and ensnared them in various schemes.

I know the New Republic doesn't like to mention it, but the Empire, for all its faults—and there were many—did try to keep this sort of petty criminal who preyed on the innocent in check. Once the Rebellion started, chaos reigned everywhere, and the O'Kenoby gang, riding around the galaxy in the Century Turkey, a rattling piece of junk held together with gum and wires, just had a field day.

They flew from planet to planet, working whatever opportunities they found. They cheated at podraces; faked odds at fathier tracks; ran gambling rackets so that whenever the house seemed to be losing, Chewie pounded his chest and growled at the unfortunate player. They took money for smuggling jobs and never delivered the goods, choosing instead to sell them to the highest bidder. There was no dishonest way to make a living that they didn't try at least once.

It was Benny O'Kenoby, the wily leader, who came up with their longest-running scheme. They claimed that Clodplodder had learned the secrets of the Jedi, that mysterious ancient cult, and could wield supernatural powers. They'd fly to some backwater planet, set up shop in remote villages where the inhabitants lacked quality entertainment, and put on shows that demonstrated Clodplodder's supposed abilities.

O'Kenoby and Shooter would go from house to house and tell tall tales about Luke to drum up interest. The Wookiee would parade around their little makeshift stage with painted advertisement boards sandwiching his body, and growl and moan for attention. Luke would sit on the stage and smile at the ladies, trying to entice them to come see the circus.

Their show had a few parts. There was Luke's "Jedi mind trick," a basic hypnosis gag that was much less impressive than any street busker's act on Coruscant. They had Luke juggle lit welding torches, which they painted and decorated to look like lightsabers. They had Luke fake-wrestle the Wookiee, and the Wookiee would jump around and slam into things, pretending Luke had thrown him with "the Force."

Since Luke grew up in a rural settlement just like the

ones his victims lived in, he knew exactly how to get the bored and unsophisticated villagers to bring out their credit chips.

But their most famous act was the one where they blindfolded Luke and gave him a welding torch and had hover droids shoot blaster bolts at him. Relying on his supernatural "Force" powers, Luke would deflect every blast without looking. It was a big crowd-pleaser.

"Sorry to interrupt again," said the hooded man, "but how did they pull that last one off?"

"Glad you asked," said Redy. She dipped a Naboo sardine fritter in lava sauce, dropped it into her mouth, and generously offered the plate to the rest of us as she chomped. The woman with the monkey-lizard boots took one, tentatively licked it, and blanched. I declined. The Togruta took two.

Redy swallowed and went on. "All you had to do was program the droids to shoot at the brightest moving objects. Those things were easy to hack because they were sold for civilian use and didn't have any of the security protocols found on military equipment. Then, as Luke posed and waved that welding torch around randomly, the droids would shoot at the bright arc from the 'lightsaber.' It only *looked* like he was anticipating the blasts. Any twelve-year-old who paid attention in school could have pulled that off."

"I see." The hooded man nodded. "Please, go on. I'm fascinated."

After the main show, the gang would encourage every-one to line up so Clodplodder could use "Force" powers to heal the sick, tell fortunes, prepare love potions, and so on, all for a "reasonable" fee. Chewie growled and glared at anyone who dared to express a hint of skepticism or didn't get in line quickly enough. It was half con, half robbery.

Eventually, enough victims complained that the authorities caught up to them. Although the O'Kenoby gang mostly stuck to preying on remote settlements, the Rebel Alliance wanted to make an example out of them to show that it could maintain order and keep people safe from crime, just like the Empire. Benny and his gang were arrested and taken to the rebel base on Yavin 4. A big show trial was planned, and Princess Leia Organa, one of the bigwigs in the Alliance, asked specifically to run it herself.

That was when the gang pulled off its biggest con. What I'm about to tell you is so secret that not even all the top leaders of the New Republic know the details.

In short, to avoid a lengthy prison sentence, Benny

O'Kenoby offered to put his gang's skills in the service of the Rebel Alliance.

"Listen," he said. "I know the Rebellion isn't going so well. People are losing faith in you, and the Empire is striking hard at your bases."

"Why are you telling me this?" the princess asked, all wary and suspicious-like.

"What you need is a good show to restore faith in your cause, and nobody knows showmanship better than this group," said Shooter.

"We do have a good show planned," said Leia. "We're going to try you in open court, publicize your crimes, and then make you work hard to pay back your victims—"

"No, no, no," interrupted Clodplodder. (And Chewie growled for emphasis.) "That's not a good use of your valuable and limited resources. Why try us as small-time crooks when we can do so much more for you?"

"Um, how do you know so much about what was said back then?" asked the hooded man. "Were you there?"

"Of course not," snapped Redy. "Obviously, I'm taking some poetic license for a better story."

"Ah," said the hooded man. "Poetic license. Right."

"I had to piece together what happened from rumors and clues gathered over many years and across many systems, and the reconstruction required filling in the blanks with some speculation." Redy sounded a bit defensive. "But I'm *pretty sure* I know what happened. It takes a trained mind to make the necessary leaps of logic and connect the dots from the barest hints, you get me?"

We gestured for her to go on.

Curious, the princess decided to listen to what the gang had to say, but the plan that O'Kenoby and his band came up with was so preposterous that she summarily sent everyone back to their prison cells.

But she didn't follow through with her original plan for a show trial, either.

As the Rebel Alliance's situation worsened every day, the princess returned to talk with the gang from time to time. The more she thought about their plan, the less absurd it seemed.

And to further convince her, Shooter and Clodplodder both practiced their considerable charms on the princess, and in the end, Shooter actually managed to get the princess to fall in love with him. To this day I can't imagine how he pulled that off.

Also, as I'm sure you've figured out by now, Shooter—or "General Solo," as we know him—basically owes his entire so-called career to Princess Leia. He was never any use as a leader or fighter at all. All these tales of his derring-do were just stories the New Republic government made up later to make Leia's spouse seem more *impressive and glamorous. Come on! A smuggler with a heart of gold? The layabout who suddenly finds his courage and leadership abilities because of the love of a princess? Really? Even holodramas wouldn't use such a hackneyed and ridiculous plot.*

"I've always found the Han Solo legend a bit hard to believe myself," my Togruta seatmate chimed in. "I heard rumors that he used to be a bit of a rogue and would shoot first—"

"Exactly," interrupted Redy. "But the official version from the New Republic government was purged of anything that would make him seem less than heroic. All this just goes to show you that governments are the biggest con artists of them all."

Although a few faces in the circle of benches had been showing signs of skepticism at the rest of Redy's tale, everyone nodded at this sentiment, including me. Empire, Rebel Alliance, New Republic, First Order— the one thing you learn trying to scrape out a living in space is that governments can't be trusted. Nine times out of ten, they are the problem.

"Leia really is an extraordinary individual," said the hooded man. His tone was placid, wistful. "She's certainly the smartest one in that family."

Redy gave him an odd look. "Speaking of governments and con jobs . . ."

The Empire was running a con of its own at the time. To demoralize the rebels, Imperial disinformation specialists had been spreading rumors for years that the Empire was constructing a battle station called the Death Star, which was supposed to have the power to destroy an entire planet.

Sorry, but I have to go on a tangent here. Again, as an engineer, let me tell you the Death Star is completely implausible. First, I've done the math, and there's just no way that known technology could generate that kind of power. None whatsoever. Handwavium from mystical "kyber crystals" just doesn't cut it. (I'm not even going to go into all the ways the purported design of the space station makes no engineering sense, either. You wouldn't be able to afford the number of drinks it would take for me to walk you through those.)

Second, you can't possibly construct a working superweapon like that without conducting tests. I don't care what kind of engineers and scientists you have working for you, it's just not possible. And yet, before Alderaan, there were no verified tests of the Death Star at all. Not a single one. I know that conspiracy nuts like to claim that the mining accident on Jedha was a covered-up test, but I've looked into the evidence, and all they've got is a lot of unscientific speculation, not proof.

The point is this: the Death Star was a political trick to ensure the loyalty of the moffs during that crucial phase of the war, when it was uncertain whether the Empire or the Rebel Alliance would prevail. And despite how farfetched the whole thing was, for a few years it served its propaganda purpose.

But you could keep up a lie for only so long before people started to doubt, and to shore up the lie, the Empire staged the destruction of Alderaan.

"Staged!" I exclaimed. "I had friends there. The whole world was blown up. I don't care what your engineering sense tells you. That was real!"

"I didn't say what happened to Alderaan wasn't real," Redy said. "I'm not some Imperial apologist. The massacre of the people of Alderaan, who didn't even have any weapons, was one of the greatest crimes committed by the Emperor. But it wasn't done with some super-secret battle station."

"But I saw the holos," said one of the listeners in the circle. "The Empire publicized it as a demonstration of power." We all nodded, shuddering at the memory of the footage.

"Again, you have to focus on the details," said Redy. "If you examined the footage carefully—which I've done frame by frame—you would notice that some of the shots showed just a brilliant ball of sparks while others showed an expanding ring of superheated material in space. *How could the same event have two different filmed versions?* Clearly faked."

"So what really happened?" asked the hooded man, his voice tense.

"Listen, the massacre of Alderaan was real, and so was the destruction of the planet. My personal theory is that it was done with a carefully placed series of proton torpedoes directed along tectonic-plate fault lines.

I've run the computer simulations, and it is entirely possible. Again, the math doesn't lie. The Empire decided that killing millions on that day wasn't enough. It had to turn it into a bigger lie for political intimidation. That is true evil."

We all nodded again. As men and women living beyond the borders of the law, we might have had our differences with the New Republic, but we all agreed that the Empire was cruel beyond measure.

After a moment of silence to mourn the victims of Alderaan, I asked, "What happened next?"

The destruction of Alderaan was the catalyst that finally made up Princess Leia's mind to work with the O'Kenoby gang. Her home planet had been destroyed and her people massacred by the Empire just to make a point, to make a lie last longer. It was intolerable. The Rebel Alliance had to strike back.

O'Kenoby, Shooter, Chewie, and Clodplodder had told her all along that they could help her do something about the Death Star. The conspiracy between Leia and the con men was at once cynical and audacious and ridiculous and theatrical. In other words, it was perfect.

First, the conspirators found in the history archives records of an Old Republic general named Obi-Wan Kenobi, who had disappeared years earlier during the Clone Wars. They claimed that Benny O'Kenoby was actually the same person and let it be known that Kenobi had come out of retirement. Then they said Kenobi had confronted Lord Darth Vader, the Emperor's right-hand man, in an old-fashioned duel and was killed. This gave the Rebel Alliance a hero and a martyr at once, someone who could go toe to toe with the greatest warrior of the Empire. O'Kenoby took a good chunk of *credits from the Rebel Alliance and disappeared. Score one point for the rebels.*

Next, they made up a story about how the O'Kenoby gang had been on a daring raid on the actual Death Star to rescue Princess Leia, who had been imprisoned because she had managed to steal the plans for the battle station and hidden them in an astromech droid.

To make everyone sound more heroic, they gave the gang members new names, and that's how we ended up with "Luke Skywalker," "Han Solo," and "Chewbacca." Even their ship, the Century Turkey, *got a new paint job and was renamed the* Millennium Falcon.

Notice how in their story, the princess played such a critical role? Master spy! Secret agent! You'll never find a politician who can turn down a chance to claim credit, even if it's for a fake accomplishment. This gave the Rebel Alliance another victory that they trumpeted to show everyone just how well they were doing. Since there was no actual Death Star, the Empire had no way to disprove the rumors. Score another point for the rebels.

But it was the final step that revealed their pure genius. Luke Clodplodder, now known as Luke Skywalker, suggested that they destroy the Death Star.

Luke, despite his lazy boyhood, was a good hustler, and frauds always seem to have an uncanny instinct for picking out other frauds. He must have figured out that the Empire never had a Death Star to begin with and that the destruction of Alderaan by the superweapon was just a bit of smoke and mirrors intended to strike fear into the hearts of the rebels.

Luke, however, was going to turn the Empire's lies against it.

The rebels staged the entire Battle of Yavin.

Now, now, you can pick your jaws off the floor. This wasn't quite as difficult to pull off as you might imagine. The rebel base on Yavin 4 was tiny, which meant that controlling information was easy. The Yavin system was out of the way of most hyperspace trade routes, and there would be few unexpected, neutral observers. The only people who would be in a position to view the imaginary Death Star up close were a dozen or so X-wing pilots, and the promise of making them heroes through the media was enough to secure their cooperation.

Since everything was happening in space, all the conspirators had to do was project some holograms onto the command center displays to give everyone on Yavin 4 the illusion that a big battle was taking place far above them. You could tell that they didn't have much time to work up the whole thing, because the propaganda holos showed only flickering displays and simple graphics, which they blamed on primitive equipment at the base. Everyone who had a role in the plot said their lines as the graphics changed, and whoever wasn't in on the conspiracy believed it was all real.

But evidence that it was faked showed up everywhere to a trained eye. I've studied the leaked "schematics" from the Death Star, and they make no sense. Think about the exhaust port vulnerability that ended the Death Star: even a second-year engineering student at the Imperial Academy wouldn't have made that kind of mistake. And even if the mistake somehow had been made, it couldn't have survived the layers of bureaucratic assessments and simulations. Even the design for a latrine on a starship was subjected, by Imperial regulation, to seventeen rounds of engineering reviews!

I know I'm not the first to raise questions about this implausible vulnerability, and I've heard the theory that maybe it was the result of deliberate sabotage. But if you believe the ragtag Rebel Alliance was capable of infiltrating the highest echelons of the disciplined Imperial military research labs, I've got a few choice plots of beachfront property I'd like to sell you on Tatooine.

Regardless of how sloppy the faked destruction of the Death Star was, the rebels did make up a perfect story to go with the victory. It didn't matter if the story wasn't true. It felt true. The crowd wanted it to be true.

It was an old-fashioned, nail-biting drama of the scrappy underdog overcoming impossible odds. Luke's "miracle shot" was the result of his Jedi Force sense and incredible piloting skills. Solo and Chewie played supporting roles with a last-minute change of heart. And the victory, of course, only happened because of the bravery and wise leadership of Princess Leia, the greatest spy and military strategist in the whole galaxy—incidentally laying the foundation for her future rise to the rank of general. It was exactly the kind of story the despairing rebels needed, and Luke and Leia delivered.

They filmed a model exploding in a dark room for the finale. And by piling up a few derelict space barges and junk station modules around Yavin 4 and having the X-wings blow them to smithereens, the Rebel Alliance generated whatever debris was needed to round out the lie.

The Battle of Yavin was a propaganda disaster for

the Empire. Their fake battle station was destroyed in an imaginary battle, but what could the Empire do? Admit that they had been lying about all of it? Conjure an actual Death Star out of thin air? They had to swallow the defeat and admit that they were conned by a smarter crook.

(They did respond by trying to build an actual, for-real Death Star later, but that also didn't happen quite the way it's been told. I'll save that story for another time.)

Yavin was also the beginning of the legend of Luke Skywalker, Jedi Knight. The Rebel Alliance milked it for every bit it was worth. He became a hero in just about every major battle of the Rebellion, and they showed his handsome mug every chance they got. Soon people began to tell stories about this chosen one, the farm-boy hero, and the Skywalker myth took on a life of its own.

More and more systems rebelled to join the Alliance after the staged battle. The Empire reeled from a shrinking tax base, and tons of Imperial support staff had to be let go. I was one of the casualties of that bureaucratic shrinkage. And I've made it my mission since then to find out the truth of what happened.

Redy drained the last mouthful of her spice tea and ate the last Naboo sardine fritter, a satisfied twinkle in her eyes.

We were all a bit too shocked to speak. Eventually, I ventured, "Did you . . . did you ever try to publish your findings?"

Redy shook her head. "How could I? This conspiracy goes to the highest levels of the New Republic government. Even Mon Mothma must be in on it. No one will believe me. And what would be the point? The New Republic has turned out to be better for just about everyone, and no one wants to know that their heroes aren't real. All I can do is share the truth with my fellow spacers who prefer to live outside the reach of the long arm of the law."

"Do you know what happened to Luke Skywalker later?" the hooded man asked. "I heard that he disappeared."

"That he did," said Redy. "My guess is that he got bored with living as a hero and decided to go back to practicing his old tricks. I've heard tales from all over the galaxy of a stranger who wields a lightsaber and performs miracles for the downtrodden. That's probably him conning unsophisticated villagers again."

The hooded man laughed, a deep, sincere-sounding expression of mirth. "I think that is one of the most interesting stories I've ever heard, and that is really saying something, given my life. Thank you."

Redy nodded, clearly pleased.

The hooded man turned to the droid bartender. "Could I trouble you to recharge this portable energy block at the highest power setting? I'm in a hurry to get back to my droid." He handed a small cube and a credit chip to the droid, who scurried behind the bar.

"I think I'm still a *little* hungry," said Redy.

We in the circle looked at one another and smiled. Some cons are fun to fall for.

"I'll buy you another plate of fritters," said the Togruta.

"But you have to tell another story," said the woman with the monkey-lizards on her boots.

"Oh, I've got plenty of stories!" said a grinning Redy. She turned to the droid bartender. "A *quadruple* shot, extra-extra bubbles, *all* your blue milk powder—and get me another plate of Naboo sardine fritters . . . but up the heat with *magma* sauce. These other two are paying." She turned back to the rest of us. "Speaking of Naboo sardine fritters, did you know that Senator Jar Jar Binks and Lord Vader were the same person?"

As Redy's audience gasped and whistled appreciatively, the bartender wheeled back to deliver Redy her food and drink.

The man got up and reached for the power cube in its charging cradle behind the bar.

"Not yet!" The bartender's head spun around as the droid chided the man. "The hyperload charger has to cool off."

Having touched a quick-charged energy cube once by mistake, I knew the bartender wasn't just being fussy. Those things could burn the skin off your hand if they hadn't cooled down. That's why typically only droids handled them.

The man wrapped his fingers around the cube, as though he hadn't heard.

"Wait!" I jumped up to stop him. But I knew it was already too late.

Instead of screaming in pain, however, he simply

thanked the droid and turned to me with a smile, holding up the energy block.

He was wearing a plain black glove over his right hand, but I couldn't imagine how such thin material could afford him enough protection.

The man nodded at the circle of patrons and turned to leave the Dande Donjon. The rest of the customers, already absorbed in Redy's latest tale, barely glanced up. I, on the other hand, left my seat and followed.

He was already halfway across the broad expanse of green, heading toward the line of spaceships parked at the shore. "Wait!" I shouted. He stopped, turned around, and waited for me to catch up.

He removed his hood, and his face seemed familiar to me somehow. I stared at his scruffy, travel-worn face and twinkling eyes. "Do you . . . do you know something about the events in Redy's story?"

He gazed at me placidly. "Let's say that I do."

"Was any of what she said true?"

He chuckled. "Let's say that some of my friends would not agree with that particular version."

"Then why didn't you correct her?"

His gaze was so intense that it seemed as if he were looking into my soul. "Why would I have done that?"

"To defend the reputations of the heroes of the New Republic! Of . . . Luke Skywalker."

"The heroes of the New Republic didn't think of themselves as heroes. They thought of themselves as ordinary men and women who did what had to be done to restore freedom and justice to the galaxy. For me to challenge her would have been giving in to fear, fear that their reputations, rather than their deeds, were what mattered. It would have led to anger, anger that they were not worshipped by everyone who benefited from their sacrifices. It would have led to hate, hate that the truth was not enough by itself. But that would have been giving in to the dark side."

I thought about his words and my life, the moments

when I had given in to fear, anger, hate. I didn't know what to say. I wanted to ask him for more.

But he raised his hand in a gesture of benediction and said, "You will go back now to enjoy another story and refreshing spice tea."

The wind by the shore was chilly, and nothing in the world seemed more wonderful than wrapping my hands around a warm mug and hearing Redy tell another outrageous tale.

"I will go back now to enjoy another story and refreshing spice tea," I said.

The man smiled, put up his hood, and walked away.

INTERLUDE ONE

THE SPECIES-SPECIFIC EXPRESSIONS of disbelief had been growing steadily on the faces of the deckhands as they watched Dwoogan efficiently wipe up the galley counter while recounting her tale. When she was finally done, a wave of riotous shouts broke out.

"Oh, come on! That's ridiculous!"

"Redy doesn't know what she's talking about!"

"TWWWWEEEEE! THPFFFFTTTT WEEEEE!"

"Who was that man in the hood?"

Dwoogan rinsed out the washcloth in the sink, chuckling the whole while.

"You asked for a story," she said. "Don't blame the teller if the story isn't quite what you were expecting."

"But . . . but . . ." Teal, who had made it back in time

to catch most of Dwoogan's story, struggled to find words. "Redy thinks everything the New Republic has been saying is a lie!"

"Every story is true to the teller," said Dwoogan. "That doesn't mean they're all equally true in the larger sense. The only way to tell what is true in the grand scheme of things is to listen to lots of stories."

"Hearing stories you don't like can be a good thing. It reminds you that not everyone thinks alike," said Ulina. "The Empire wanted everyone to think alike, remember? In fact, Luke and the heroes of the New Republic fought so that people like Redy can tell their stories without fearing for their lives. She might be fined for being an unlicensed engineer, but the authorities won't ever jail her for her stories. That's a good thing."

The deckhands pondered this.

Ulina was about to tell everyone to head to their

bunks when G'kolu piped up: "I wonder what an Imperial soldier would think of Luke Skywalker."

Tyra looked uncomfortable at this. She had always seemed to be extra wary of New Republic customs officials and safety inspectors whenever the *Wayward Current* was in dock, preferring to stay out of sight. Though it was the rule among the deckhands not to pry into each other's pasts, a few suspected that her family had some kind of connection with the Empire. Several deckhands glanced at Tyra curiously, but the girl avoided their eyes.

Dwoogan broke in smoothly. "Ha, they've got some fun tales. You just have to get them real drunk first. They're not all bad sorts. Some of them fought for the Empire because they weren't told any other stories."

Tyra said nothing, but she gave Dwoogan a grateful smile as the other deckhands seized on the opening the cook had provided.

"Tell us a story from an Imperial!"

"Tell us!"

"Yeah!"

Dwoogan nodded at Ulina. "Ask your third mate. She used to help Imperials who wanted to get out of that life find jobs with smuggling crews."

The deckhands turned to Ulina with even more awe and admiration in their eyes.

Ulina's glowing eye patch shifted through a range of hues, from deep turquoise to brilliant vermillion, as she pondered the request. "Uniforms can be deceiving—both to the wearers and to those looking at them. Many of the stories I know aren't safe to share. The New Republic may have forgiven those who took off their Imperial uniforms, but there are still some who have not."

The deckhands looked thoughtful. Certainly they all had secrets that they didn't want the others to know; it was why they had chosen or been swept into this life beyond the law. Tyra bit her bottom lip and nodded almost imperceptibly.

Ulina looked at Tyra. Abruptly, she asked, "You've been to Jakku, right?"

Surprised, Tyra locked eyes with Ulina. "My family are scavengers, and I was there with them for a while." She swallowed. "We . . . we couldn't get other jobs."

"Did you see the starship graveyard?" asked Ulina.

Tyra's eyes lit up. "Oh, yes. The wrecks were magnificent. My grandmother used to take me to where she—to explore the officers' quarters on some of the big destroyers."

"So let me tell you a story about Luke Skywalker and the starship graveyard."

"I didn't know he was on Jakku!"

"Well, you'll see. The story I'm about to tell you has been passed from teller to teller across many smuggling crews. The original teller was someone who fought for the Emperor. . . ."

Ulina's voice changed, and even her face seemed to take on the appearance of another as she began to recount the tale from the perspective of its first teller.

ALWAYS REMEMBER: YOUR FOCUS
DETERMINES YOUR REALITY.

—QUI-GON JINN

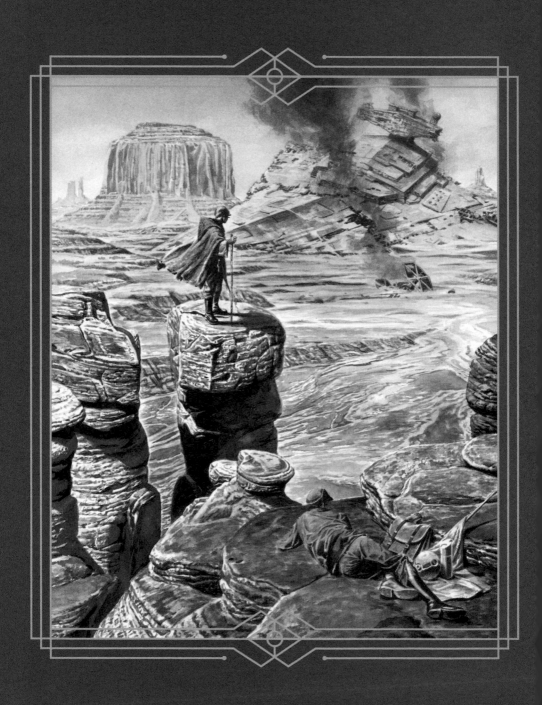

THE STARSHIP GRAVEYARD

I LIVED UNDER THE GLORIOUS REIGN of Emperor Palpatine. I lived to see the New Republic's petty leaders squabble over the ashes of a once-great galaxy. I lived, but my comrades died.

The Battle of Jakku is celebrated today as the final defeat of the Galactic Empire, but for me, it was both my first and last tour of duty as a gunner aboard a Star Destroyer in the Imperial Navy. I was a young man of twenty, dedicated to the Emperor's cause of bringing order to the galaxy.

The life of a gunner is one of endless waiting punctuated by flashes of terror.

Waiting . . . waiting . . . waiting . . . my fingers tense over the console, heart pounding, sweat dripping . . . *there*, flashing streaks over the starboard bow! Target, track, fire! Waiting . . . waiting . . . waiting . . . the voice of the computer echoing around the vast bridge as banks of consoles blinked in the semidarkness under the stars, illuminating terrified faces, each as young as mine.

Green as I was, even I knew the battle wasn't going well.

The Empire had gathered practically every capital ship into orbit around Jakku, and the rebels, bent on chaos and disruption, had converged to the same corner of space with their ragtag fleet. This was to be a textbook grand battle, a confrontation between the good of order and the evil of anarchy.

True to our commitment to discipline, the Imperial ships fell into neat ranks and tight formations. True to their despicable worship of chaos, the rebels followed no code of tactics or rules of engagement. They swept around our flanks, skimmed over our blind spots, refused to engage us head-on.

A series of explosions against the bridge. Bright lights blinded us momentarily. We were hit. Hard.

The deck lurched, men and women spilled out of their chairs, the viewscreens and windows tilted and jumped crazily, showing glimpses of wildly spinning stars and the long glowing arc of the desert planet below us.

"Losing altitude," intoned the computer. Klaxons blared. "Velocity vectors incompatible with stable orbit."

We were falling toward the planet, unable to climb out of the deadly trap of its gravity well.

My crewmates and I struggled up as the deck stabilized and officers barked orders. Outside the windows, we could see the massive bow start to glow orange from friction against the upper reaches of the atmosphere.

The deck buckled again, and we screamed and tumbled back down.

My head struck a console as I fell, and blood streamed down my face, blurring my vision. Through the haze of blood and sweat and terror, I saw a glowing hologram rotating over the console.

MOST WANTED: LUKE SKYWALKER, JEDI WAR CRIMINAL, EXTREMELY DANGEROUS

The internal channel broadcasting the holo was dedicated to showing the likenesses and crimes of the most dangerous rebels. In regular operation, the channel had the effect of raising our alertness against rebel infiltration. But now, as I lay on the ground, it was terrifying to see the image of this hooded Jedi terrorist slowly spinning against the stars, looming over me like a sneering monster.

My heart skipped a beat as the deck lurched again. Amid the screams and a shower of sparks, peering through the hologram, I focused on the main windows of the bridge. A powerful bolt of energy arced across space to strike an Imperial Star Destroyer. The angle of the spinning Skywalker made it seem as if the hologram were floating in space, and the dazzling bolt had shot out of his fingertips.

I was not a superstitious man, but I shuddered at that horrid image.

Instantly, glowing cracks appeared in the dark gray hull, and the struck destroyer seemed to groan in pain in the silence of space.

Like an ancient ocean-going vessel taking on water, the dagger-shaped ship dipped and fell toward the surface of Jakku. Faster and faster it fell, and the gray vessel glowed red, then orange, and finally bright white as it plunged into the thick atmosphere toward its death far below.

My heart convulsed as I imagined the voices howling for mercy in that doomed ship.

Like some angry and capricious god, the hologram of the Jedi spun as two more bright streaks seemed to shoot out of him. The bolts crossed the span of bridge windows and struck two more Imperial Star Destroyers. Slowly disintegrating, the ships dove into the roiling ocean of air below like fallen Corosian phoenixes, their TIE squadrons swerving aimlessly in space, as helpless as orphaned hatchlings.

It was a sign. It was a nightmare. It had to mean *something*.

Beams of lightning crisscrossed the windows and ensnared more Imperial Star Destroyers. Like lassoed beasts, the graceful, dark metallic hulks buckled and strained against the tractor beams. But their struggles were useless. One by one, the ships lost their momentum, dipped, and were hurled down toward Jakku.

I did not see any rebel star cruisers that could have launched the beams. In fact, the shots all seemed to terminate in the steadily spinning hologram of the Jedi, his machine of death, that red-striped X-wing, hovering over him like a trained bird of prey or a magician's familiar.

Carelessly, almost lazily, the hologram turned to face me, and stopped moving.

I gasped. Instead of a face I saw only a bright, featureless oval under the glowing hood. The holographic circuits sputtered and hissed, and an acrid smell filled my nostrils. Interference artifacts appeared in the projection. The hologram's hands reached toward me, as though intent on grabbing my throat.

Before I could scream, the holographic projector failed, and the Jedi winked out of existence in a bright electronic explosion.

Behind where the hologram had been, I saw that the bridge windows were rapidly filling with expanding columns of energy.

"Shields collapsing," intoned the computer. "Hull breach imminent. Brace for impact. Brace. Brace—"

A jolt, as though the entire Star Destroyer had been picked up by a giant hand and slammed against the ground. My teeth and bones rattled. My vision swam. My ears filled with a high-pitched, incessant drone.

The bridge went dark: the overhead lights, the viewscreens, the blinking lights on the banks of consoles, even the emergency lighting strips in the floor. All around us was the darkness of space; the faint, heartless glow of distant stars; and the dim radiance of heated, thin upper-atmosphere air against the bridge windows.

My ears popped. Then I heard the inhuman, deafening metallic roar and screech of a ship dying in space.

The gravity generators failed, and we experienced

the sensation of free fall as our bodies lifted off the deck.

My crewmates and I screamed until we could not catch our breaths. The noise no longer sounded like living screams but an eerie replacement for the throbbing of the engines, which had suddenly been silenced.

The ship slowed, drifted, stopped, and then the stark, lifeless surface of Jakku swung into view, filling the windows, and we fell.

We fell.

Scrambling, shoving, kicking, somehow I made my way to one of the escape pods and strapped myself in. The only thought in my mind before I lost consciousness amid the screeching and groaning of struts and bulkheads strained to their limits was this:

We couldn't have lost; we shouldn't have lost; this was not a fair fight.

The heat of a thousand suns. Unbearable thirst. Pain like I had never endured.

My eyes opened to the grimace of a woman wearing the black uniform cap of the Imperial Navy. I didn't recognize her. I tried to speak but only a croak emerged from my parched throat. I stared into her eyes, willing her to respond.

I took in her cracked lips, her bloodied chin, her—

My mind wanted to flee from the sight, but my body would not respond.

The face belonged to a head that was not attached to a body. It sat on the glittering desert sand like a cactus. The sand under the head was a dark crimson.

All around me were scattered pieces from the wreckage of the escape pod and bodies twisted into impossible positions. Acrid smoke. Waves of heat from still burning debris. Corpses and more corpses.

I tried to scream but could not catch my breath. I blacked out again.

We couldn't have lost; we shouldn't have lost.

I was back in space, a disembodied consciousness observing the battle from somewhere in high orbit, the all-powerful Imperial fleet drifting beneath me, an army of giants being nipped at by underpowered rebel star cruisers and their swarming fighters.

And the hologram Jedi was there, too.

No, not a hologram. He was real, a glowing figure of sorcery and magic. He floated in space, his feet astride the stars, his cape billowing with an arcane power that could not be understood by mere mortals.

He leapt from rebel star cruiser to rebel star cruiser, his flaming sword at the ready. A Star Destroyer focused all its cannons on him, and carelessly, he deflected the shots with graceful swings. He launched himself from a cruiser, tucked his legs under him, and tumbled through space, shooting bolts of energy from his sword in every direction. Star Destroyer after Star Destroyer disintegrated under this unnatural assault.

It was impossible. It was unbelievable. Yet it was true. The Jedi was dispatching capital ships with his sword of magic alone.

Tired of his game, the Jedi suddenly put away his shining sword. He swung his arms and reached for the Imperial fleet with his bare hands, and thin strands of crackling energy emerged from his palms like a fishing net cast into the ocean that was the galaxy. The glowing strands reached the ships and ensnared them, and the Jedi laughed like a child playing by the sea. Hauling the ships in like so many flopping fish, he cast them down toward Jakku. He was a god playing with toys, except that the toys were city-sized structures of steel and held tens of thousands of lives.

This is why we lost.

He has come, the avenging Jedi who can cast starships down from the heavens with a sword of light.

I opened my eyes and shivered. I was lying down, and it was cold, very cold.

And dark.

Overhead the stars twinkled mercilessly, like the eyes of a universe that didn't care that hundreds of thousands had just died. The galaxy had been there long before we were born, and it would be there long after we were gone.

I realized that I was moving, drifting through the sea of stars.

Have I died? Is this the afterlife?

Against the dim moonlight and starglow, a massive edifice loomed into my view on the left. It was lit here and there, offices or suites occupied by those who had not gone to sleep.

What city am I in? On what planet?

I noticed that the lights didn't hold the steady glow

of electricity, but flickered and sparked. Fire. Parts of the building were on fire. A passing breeze brought the odor of burning plastoid and insulation. The shape of the building grew more familiar. . . .

The edifice was the wreck of a fallen Star Destroyer, now resembling some giant's sword left behind, plunged into the sands of an abandoned battlefield.

I struggled to lift my head, to look around.

Three or four more Star Destroyers and star cruisers filled the view, mountains of steel and despair, a graveyard of Imperial glory. Pieces of smaller broken spacecraft and ground vehicles littered the landscape. It was a nightmarish vision drawn from fairy tales, a dark, burning forest through which I crawled like a tiny ant.

No, not crawled. *I'm being dragged.*

I was lying on a litter made from the thin terminal struts and broken partitions of a starship, lashed together. Cushions from an escape pod, still smelling of melted plastoid and smoke, provided a bit of padding. My legs were tied to splints, and the waves of pain as the litter jerked unevenly across the desert sand told me that they were broken. Heavy bandages wrapped around my thighs and waist hid injuries I did not want to see. My arms were tied to the sides of the litter, and more strips of cloth secured my waist against the frame. Near my feet lay a few sacks, and I could see broken circuit boards, sensor heads, computer modules sticking out of the openings. Also lashed to the litter next to my thighs were a few water canteens and bundles of rations.

Ahead of me, a human figure wrapped in flowing robes strained to pull me forward with the cables looped over his shoulders.

"Who are you?" I croaked.

He stopped and turned around. There wasn't enough

light for me to see his face. His hair was cut in a short, efficient style, and I could tell that he was quite thin under those billowing robes.

"I found you," he said. "You were the only one who was alive in that pod."

"There will be a reward if you bring me back to an Imperial Navy outpost."

He chuckled. "I have no love for the Empire."

A rebel then. Just my luck.

"What do you want with me?" I asked.

"Want with you?" he seemed to find this question funny. "What does one living being want with another in the desert? There are only a few answers. It isn't hard to figure out."

He turned around and leaned into the hauling cables. The litter jerked forward.

"Let me go," I whispered hoarsely.

Either he didn't hear me or he didn't care. He simply plodded on. One step. Then another.

A wave of dizziness and nausea washed over me. I was his prisoner, and there was nothing I could do.

His robe looks just like the glowing garment worn by that Jedi.

I stopped straining, fell back, and let myself drift back to sleep.

When I was a child, my mother told me dark tales of ancient wizards who wielded magic to bring the fire of the stars to sentient species, and of villains who cast spells to twist living worlds into dry husks. In those stories, merely escaping from the clutches of the powerful magicians made you a hero.

I took a sip from the canteen. My arms were no longer tied to the sides of the litter. I ached all over and some infection had taken hold in my blood, making me feverish and tired. I needed a clinic, or a medical droid. No functioning version of either existed as far as I could see.

But my legs felt better, or at least numb, and I believed that if I had to I could get up and stumble a few steps.

"You can grab on to the litter yourself now," he had said when he first untied my arms, perhaps trying to make me think he had shackled me only so I wouldn't fall off. Villains, of course, never told you their true intentions.

At least my captor wasn't trying to deny me the basic necessities of life, though I had no idea what his plans for me were. "Where are you from?" I asked, as innocuously as I could manage.

"The same place all of us are from," he said. He swept his arm across the horizon. I didn't know what he meant. The sky? The desert? The looming hulks of starships?

"Where are we going?"

"The same place all of us are going." He pointed to the distance, and I didn't know if he meant some mystical realm or a concrete destination.

We had been hiking through that valley in the shadows of dead starships for days. From time to time, the man would leave my litter in the shade of some wreck while he went to investigate the metallic mountains, still full of burning craters and holes smoking like active volcanoes. I would watch him, climbing along sheer deck cliffs and traipsing across precariously balanced struts like some flea bouncing on the body of a giant luggabeast.

I learned to appreciate the beauty of the desert. Contrary to my initial impression, it wasn't a place devoid of life. Patches of flowering plants stubbornly poked out of the sand dunes, as did twisty, spiny trees. Wild steelpeckers hopped or skimmed across the dunes, their metallic beaks glinting in the sun as they headed for the carcasses of the Star Destroyers, a feast of carrion to them.

Or maybe these were just hallucinations conjured by my feverish brain. Reality seemed indistinguishable from nightmare in this world.

After an hour or two, he would return, sometimes empty-handed but often carrying pieces of machinery or electronics he had salvaged.

"Didn't see other survivors," he said. "If there were any, I hope they were as lucky as you."

So he was looking for other prisoners.

What does one living being want with another in the desert?

To eat them, to use them, to sustain one's own life at their expense. To take pleasure in their suffering.

I recalled the words in the training holos we had been shown back on the Star Destroyer. *Rebels create chaos and pain.* They would torture me even if I was only a lowly gunner who knew nothing about grand Imperial battle plans or any other secrets they wanted.

He stuffed the latest prizes from his excursion into the bags at my feet.

"More scavengers will come soon," he said, surveying the starships. I wasn't sure if he was referring to the steelpeckers or people like himself.

"What do you look for?" I asked, trying to draw him into conversation that would lower his guard.

He didn't answer. Instead, he gazed at the wreckage of an AT-AT some distance to the south, off to the side of our course. Besides the massive mountains formed by the fallen starships, the desert was full of wrecked skiffs, TIE fighters, AT-ATs, bombers, and every other kind of vehicle the Empire or the Rebel Alliance had thrown into the fighting around Jakku. The battle seemed so long before and so far away now that my life had been reduced to pining for the next sip of water or bite of rations in an endless sea of sand.

"Those things have more independent systems," he muttered to himself. "Better salvage . . . Ah, there's a nice hole blasted in the leg." He turned to me. "Might as well take a nap. I'll be gone a little longer than usual."

I watched him make his way slowly through the shimmering hot air to the AT-AT. He disappeared from view. I waited a few moments longer.

This was my chance.

I grabbed all the canteens and looped the straps around my neck. I stuffed all the remaining ration bars down the waistband of my tattered uniform. After a moment of hesitation, I took out one ration bar and put it back into my captor's sack, and dropped one canteen back onto the litter.

I heaved myself off the litter and began to crawl away. No point in putting my weight on my legs unless I had to. I was in very bad shape from the infection.

My head throbbed; my body was racked by chills. I wasn't sure I could stand up without blacking out.

About four hundred meters away, the hull of an Imperial Interdictor stood up from the desert. If I could get to it and climb inside, I was certain that I could find someplace to hide where my captor would never find me. After all, I was a trained Imperial naval gunner, and I knew where all the access conduits and crawl spaces were on a ship. I practically grew up in the military after my parents died in a rebel raid. An Imperial ship was the closest thing to a home for me.

After an arduous crawl of a hundred meters or so, I stopped to catch my breath. Normally, I could have covered the distance in less than fifteen seconds at an easy run, but the crawl had taken at least ten minutes and all my strength. I risked a look back. There was still no sign of my captor. A large, dark cloud swirled on the horizon like a living wall. The steelpeckers stopped their feeding and froze on the highest points of the hull like so many sailors standing on the deck of a starship in dock, ready for an admiral's inspection. They gazed at the dark cloud silently.

The sight was eerie, but I wasn't scared. If a storm was coming, that could only help me. Not only would the rain provide me more water, the most precious resource on a desert planet, but it would erase the tracks I'd made in the sand as I crawled to freedom.

The sun beat down on the back of my neck. I was already sunburnt, my skin blistering in places. I focused on the Interdictor and forced my arms to pull my body forward, one centimeter at a time. I had to get away from that devious man who spoke in riddles. The Imperial holos had made it clear what happened to loyal soldiers of the Empire in the hands of the merciless rebels. Especially *that* rebel, if he was who I thought he was. I shuddered at the thought of the kind of mental probes and tortures a Jedi could put me through before he was satisfied that I had no valuable intelligence.

Only a few meters more now.

I looked back again. The clouds were bigger, darker, more menacing. The last of the steelpeckers scrambled inside the wrecks like maggots burrowing into carcasses. They avoided the parts of the ships where smoke still billowed. It wasn't clear how long the fires would continue to burn. The ships were massive.

A sense of dread seized my throat. I tried to swallow and couldn't.

Hurry, hurry! I told myself. I tossed away the heavy, sloshing canteens. They were weighing me down, and the storm would bring me water. The ration bars had been pulverized during my strenuous crawl and the crumbs scattered to the wind and the sand.

Not the best-planned escape. My Imperial survival trainer would have been ashamed.

Desperately summoning all my strength, I scrambled across the last few meters between myself and the Imperial cruiser. It loomed over me like one of those magnificent towers on Coruscant, and I longed for the refuge I would find within.

With my legs basically useless, I couldn't climb too high. Instead, I made my way to one of the small thruster nozzles midship. It was over five meters across, giving me more than enough room to hide from the coming storm. I pulled myself up inside the cone-shaped nozzle as if crawling into the ear of a giant. I was soaked in sweat. Panting, my tongue parched, I wished I had kept one of the canteens with me.

But at least I was feeling safe for the first time in days. Relief flooded through me, relaxing my taut nerves and tensed muscles. The security of solitude was as sweet as blue milk, and I wanted nothing more than to fall asleep.

Imagining the refreshing rain that would soon come, I smiled.

The space inside the nozzle darkened. My heart leapt into my throat. The man's figure blocked all light.

"You'll be dead in another ten minutes if you stay here," he said. "Come on. Enough fooling around."

Throwing me over his shoulder, he dropped down from the nozzle. Then he secured me to his back with a sling and climbed slowly up the hull until he found a jagged opening. Struggling with my weight, he stumbled into the ship. We were inside a utility cabin intended for miscellaneous supplies. Unceremoniously, he dumped me onto a storage ledge.

"Are you going to behave or do I have to tie you down again?" he asked, breathing heavily.

I shook my head; I was done running.

He left and returned sometime later with the litter. As I lay recovering on the ledge, he maneuvered the litter to block the hole we had climbed through. He lashed the makeshift door to the frame of the cruiser with the hauling cables. Aided by the light of a salvaged emergency lamp, he piled pieces of debris on the litter to weigh it down, sealing the seams between it and the hull with pieces of melted plastoid and bundles of cloth.

It was almost completely dark inside the cabin. Only a few thin rays of light fell through some holes made by the steelpeckers high above us. They penetrated the murk feebly, like forlorn hope scattered by a dark sea of despair.

Outside, an otherworldly moan grew steadily until it turned into a screeching howl, followed by the staccato *pit-pat-pat* of rain lashing against the steel hull. The tiny explosions blended into a constant, resonant clang in our dark sanctuary.

It no longer sounded like rain. It sounded like a regiment of stormtroopers firing their blasters against the wrecked ship.

"A sandstorm," the man said.

I imagined myself in the nozzle outside, pounded by the suffocating sand. I imagined my skin being scoured away by a thousand wind-whipped grains. I imagined myself as a skeleton reclining in the nozzle, my bones picked clean by animals and bleached by the sun.

"How did you find me?" I croaked.

"You've been in those clothes for more than a week now," he said. "I could smell you from half a kilometer away. At least I managed to recover the water you stole."

Not magic then. Maybe this planet robbed him of magic just as it drained the life out of the starships that crashed into it.

"Did you grow up around here?" I asked. "Was that how you knew about sandstorms?"

"I grew up in a desert," he said. "One very much like this one. You need to eat. And drink."

I guzzled greedily from the canteen he held to my mouth. He pulled the last ration bar out of his sack, handed it to me, and dropped the empty sack on the floor. Lying down on the other ledge in the storage cabin, he turned his back to me and went to sleep.

In the dark tales told by my mother, the heroes needed to understand the villains to defeat them. Knowledge was the first step to control, to power, to order.

I needed to know this man who had taken me prisoner, and who had also rescued me from a sandstorm and handed me the last of his food. I needed to know this man who terrified me, but who also intrigued me.

I had seen the wanted posters, the shaky holo footage. I recalled the shiny figure on the deck of the rebel cruiser, pulling Imperial starships out of the sky with his bare hands. I remembered the way he had struggled up the wreckage with me tied to his back, refusing to abandon me to certain death. Maybe he just wanted to save me for some dark purpose later—or maybe not. I thought I knew all there was to know about this man, but in fact, I knew nothing.

After the sandstorm, we resumed our journey.

I lost count of how many starships we passed, their funeral pyres still burning. Since we had no more rations, we ate bitter roots he dug from the dunes and tiny voles he trapped with a net woven from delicate Imperial ion-conducting wires. Sometimes he cooked the meat; other times, we tore the flesh from the bones with our bare teeth. My stomach cramped from this barbaric diet.

We began to climb a hill, and the man had to stop every few steps to catch his breath.

It was hard to reconcile the figure of this man— mortal, weak, *ordinary*—with the glimpse of the powerful Jedi I had caught on the bridge of my ship. Had I imagined it all? Before the endless, unyielding sand dunes, everyone was equal, whether you were a magician or just a common soldier.

He stopped again, but this time, instead of resting, he turned to me, uncapped a canteen, and pushed the spigot against my lips.

I shook my head and moved my face away. The water, after baking in the heat of the sun for so many days, tasted bitter and metallic. Drinking it made me want to throw up.

"You haven't drunk for more than an hour now," he said. "I know you feel terrible, but dehydration is going to make it worse."

In truth, I was feeling close to death. My vision blurred and swam. The fever was so intense that I imagined myself not too different from the burning wrecks we passed. I closed my eyes so the world would stay still.

I couldn't breathe.

My eyes snapped open. He had pinched my nostrils shut. What manner of torture was this?

Panicking, I opened my mouth to gulp some air. He waited until I had taken a breath before forcing the spigot of the canteen between my teeth. I bit down but it was impossible to keep it out. He had pushed it in too far.

"Drink," he growled. "Or I'll start pouring and you can drown for all I care."

I nodded. He let go. I swallowed the bitter, foul liquid. I had no doubt that he was willing to carry out his threat. A rebel, especially a Jedi, was capable of any act of cruelty.

After I drank, he resumed pulling me up the steep side of the dune again.

"I need a doctor," I gasped. It was shameful for an Imperial soldier to beg, but I was beyond shame now.

"I know."

I swayed back and forth as he dragged me toward the bright sky. I looked back at the graveyard of starships. They shimmered in the heat. Maybe soon I was going to join them, and all my dead comrades.

"There is a place surrounded by walls beyond the dune," he said. In my semicomatose state, his voice sounded far away, unreal. "It's guarded by stormtroopers, and I've heard rumors that masked soldiers in crimson robes patrol there from time to time. I'm taking you there."

I couldn't speak. So he was planning an assault on an Imperial stronghold. Was he hoping to use me as a hostage? Surely he knew that would be useless. In the Imperial Navy, we were trained to treat hostages exactly the same as hostage takers because they were weak and allowed themselves to be used as shields. I wanted to tell him that he would gain no advantage by dragging me along.

But my slow mind finally caught the import of his words. If the compound he spoke of was guarded by stormtroopers and the Emperor's Royal Guard, then it was likely an important fortress—the fact that I hadn't heard of it probably meant it was secret. Even a Jedi would not have an easy time breaching the defenses of such a place.

I could still redeem myself by sabotaging his attack.

And if I should somehow survive, there would be doctors, medical droids, fresh water, safety.

Hope, which I thought was already dead, flickered to life deep in my mind.

With a final lurch, we crested the dune and gazed down the other side.

He had not lied. The walled compound sat in the desert like a black crown. The walls were interrupted at regular intervals by watchtowers. I strained to catch a glimpse of the imposing stormtroopers, but we were too far away.

The man sat down on the litter next to my feet. He untied a pair of long poles that ended in flat paddles. I knew what they were: blades from an air-circulating pump installed on starships. He placed the poles over his knees like the oars of a rowboat and stuck the flat paddles into the sand.

"Let's go," he said, and shoved hard.

We slid down the great sand wave on the litter raft, and he wielded the oars nimbly, giving us more speed when he thought we needed it, and steering us out of the way of protruding animal skeletons and clumps of vegetation when they got close.

Faster and faster we sailed. It was the most exhilarating and strange ride of my life.

I readied myself for a desperate burst of exertion as soon as Imperial guards came into view. I would push him off the litter and scream for help, to let the stormtroopers know that I was loyal, that I had not been rendered helpless by this dangerous war criminal, that they could still rescue me.

But no hopeful white armor showed on the walls as we approached. The doors to the compound were wide open, and a few men and women, pulling litters much like the one I was on, emerged with heaps of stolen goods.

The last of my pride and resistance left me; I wept helplessly.

Another burnt-out room. Smashed electronics, fragments of memory cores, the smoking wreckage left behind by explosive charges designed to erase all traces of the work that had been done in the laboratory.

From time to time, I heard the voices of men and women raised in anger somewhere in the compound. Scavengers fighting over scraps.

The man returned. One look at his face told me all I needed to know.

Then he picked up the hauling cables and dragged me through the maze of tiled corridors and empty laboratories again.

There were no stormtroopers, no Imperial Royal

Guards, no doctors or functioning medical droids. Whatever this facility had been, the occupants had abandoned it earlier in the battle and destroyed everything that couldn't be taken with them.

From time to time, we passed other scavengers hoping to find objects of value in this ghost compound. They looked at us warily, and some bared their teeth or flared their neck flaps or raised their horns intimidatingly. They belonged to a hodgepodge of species, some humanoid, some avian, a few aquatic or amphibian, most unknown to me. All dressed in rags. Jakku was not a rich planet, and these were people who had never scraped together enough to leave.

The man managed to negotiate with them and exchange some of his salvage for rations. He devoured a few portions and handed the rest to me.

I shook my head. The pain was so intense that staying conscious was torture. I wanted something, anything, to put me out of my misery.

"Leave me," I muttered. "Let me die."

The man said nothing. He simply went on, pulling the litter. He stopped to look in every ruined room, searching for what I knew wouldn't be there.

We were passing one of the rooms with a narrow slit-like window when it happened. First, a bright flash that made both of us turn away. Then a deep rumbling that we felt through our bones, as well as heard. The ground heaved as though we were at sea or on the deck of a struck starship. The man fell, and anything still sitting on benches or hanging on walls crashed to the ground.

A groundquake? A volcanic eruption?

The man crawled over and dragged me into the doorway, where the frame offered some shelter. We huddled tightly, hoping that the building would not collapse on top of us.

Later, after things had calmed down, we made our way outside. The other scavengers, a few dozen in all, had gathered silently on the elevated balcony overlooking the entrance to the compound. The sight that greeted us took all words away.

The wreckage of the massive Star Destroyer that had stood a few kilometers away was gone, and in its place was a bubbling, bright-orange lake of fire. The red-hot liquid, lava-like, had spread to fill the depression among the dunes in which the compound stood. The low walls of the compound held the turbulent waves of the lake of fire back. But the sandblasted walls would not last much longer.

We were stranded in the middle of a burning lake, and the dikes were failing.

Half-asleep, I listened to the voices of the scavengers.

"The reactor cores in the ship must have suffered a meltdown. . . ."

"Lucky that no one was anywhere near it . . ."

"... not lava. That's melted sand. ..."

"... a sea of liquid glass ..."

"There are cracks in the walls already. ..."

It was night, and the cold desert air was made more tolerable by the heat emanating from the glass lake. The fiery liquid cast a dim red glow against the faces of all the scavengers. The strong wind, the result of the drastic change in temperature between the desert day and night, drove powerful ripples and waves across the surface. Surrounded by a lake of tempestuous glass and dozens of misfit creatures from all over the galaxy, I again had the sensation that I was living in a dark fairy tale spun by my mother.

"We can't stay here," said the man who had taken me there. "When the walls collapse, we'll drown in fire."

"What do you suggest we do, then?" asked one of the other scavengers. He wore a simple vest made of woven wires over his furry body, and all his prized salvage—small electronics, tools, power supplies, gleaming crystal fragments—was attached to the net vest like the haul from a strange sea.

The man had no answer. There were no functioning vehicles left in the compound, and even if there were, how could mere wheels or treads be useful in a lake of scorching liquid glass? Only an AT-AT might have a chance, but there was none to be found.

I fell asleep. I was going to die, but the great villain of the Rebellion, trapped with me, would not escape, either. That was some comfort.

When I woke up, the man was gone.

I struggled to sit up and frantically looked around.

The dejected scavengers, seeing no way to escape their fate, huddled in small groups around the balcony. They played games of chance, shared stories, or simply stared into nothing at all.

A small figure down below, on top of the walls, caught my attention.

He was strapping something flat and large to his feet. I squinted against the hot breeze coming off the surface of the lake.

They were the paddles from the air-circulating pumps.

With no warning, the figure jumped into the lake. I was too shocked to cry out.

But instead of sinking into the deadly waves, he stayed afloat. Just like the wide boots issued to Imperial soldiers in snowy terrain, the paddles acted like miniature boats that distributed his weight across a wide area. Tentatively, he took a step forward, like a long-limbed water strider floating on a puddle.

Step by step, he gained confidence. As I watched his billowing robe float over the fiery lake like a blooming lotus, I imagined the hot liquid cooling into pure, crystalline glass. I imagined him stepping across the surface as easily as a boy loping across a sheet of ice. I imagined the stars reflected in the glass, an upside-down sky over which he strode.

He was the sky walker. I almost laughed aloud at the thought. Of course he was.

"That's a ridiculous suggestion!"

"Absolutely not!"

"One slip and we'll be dead."

"You must be trying to kill us so you can steal our possessions."

"The walls are holding, I think—"

"Maybe we should try to pile up the rubble here and build a tower. Even if the walls fall—"

"Stop it!" the man shouted. The cacophony of voices died. "I know you're terrified. I am, too. But there is no other solution. You've seen the walls. They won't last much longer. Even if you try to pile up all the rubble here and build a tower high enough to survive the flood, will your rations last until the glass cools? We have to walk out of here."

The other scavengers looked skeptically at the paddles strapped to his feet. The very idea of trusting their lives to such flimsy contraptions on a burning lake was absurd.

They drifted away from the man, alone or in twos and threes to continue their hopeless games and useless fantasies. They refused to acknowledge the reality of our shared fate.

I beckoned to the man. Surprised, he leaned down to hear what I had to say.

"Tell them who you are," I whispered.

He pulled back and looked at me warily. I beckoned to him again.

"I know the truth," I said. "I saw you up there"—I pointed to the stars—"and also down here. I thought you'd lost your powers. But then I saw you stride across the lake, so I know you've gotten your powers back. You're still Luke Skywalker, the Jedi. They will follow you, but you have to tell them the truth."

He sat up and looked at me with an expression I could not name. A few seconds later, the corners of his mouth curled up in a smile.

I was drifting under the stars again. Just like how I had arrived on that planet.

"Stay close to me," called Luke Skywalker. Dozens of voices acknowledged him from behind.

I strained to look back. Over the molten lake of glass, a long, serpentine caravan wound its way. In the lead was Luke Skywalker, magnificent in his glowing Jedi robes and hauling me on a litter. The paddles strapped to his feet allowed him to step high and pull me with confidence, and the shiny metallic foil—scavenged from the Imperial compound—he wore instead of the thick shawl kept him cool by reflecting the heat of the molten sand away from his body.

Behind us, the bravest souls wore paddles fashioned after those on Luke's feet. Molten glass was so dense that it was possible to float without making the paddles too bulky. They pulled small boats and rafts made from other insulating material, and those who were too fearful to walk on their own huddled inside the temporary vessels, covering themselves with more reflective foil to stay cool.

"I'm using the Force to guide you," Luke said into the darkness. "As long as you stay close to me, no harm will come to you. The Force is with us. We're one with the Force."

The others behind me repeated the mantra. They

didn't trust the contraptions that kept them afloat so much as they believed in the mystical power of the man leading them.

They had a point. After all, the same faith had allowed a group of ragtag rebels to defeat a galaxy-spanning empire.

The blazing waves from the molten glass lake lapped the shore behind us. The makeshift boats, rafts, and paddle shoes lay scattered on the sandy beach. We were safe.

It had been amazing to see the Jedi at work. He had convinced a group of timid men and women who distrusted each other to walk across a lake of fire. Maybe it was an example of those dark Jedi mind tricks. But it didn't feel dark. It felt like . . . hope.

One by one, the scavengers came to say good-bye.

They each left Luke Skywalker the most precious piece of salvage they had. Some had been recovered from the abandoned Imperial compound, others not. It wasn't exactly a payment. Closer to a token, a tribute to something grander than any of us.

"This power cell will fetch at least ten full portions. . . ."

"I had never seen these crystals before. The self-destruct charge must have missed them. If you can figure out the encryption . . ."

"This droid hand is the most intricate I've ever seen. Probably meant for the Emperor's own servants . . ."

"I don't know what this is. A compass, maybe? Found it in a case labeled 'Pillio.' Who knows where it will lead? Maybe to a place where you won't ever be hungry or worry about starships falling from the sky. . . ."

Skywalker thanked each and every one of them. When the last scavenger had left, he knelt next to the litter and handed me two pills.

"Take these," he said. "They won't do anything for the infection, but they'll take away the pain for a while. I found them in the compound commander's quarters."

I took the pills. The Jedi had not killed me so far, but maybe this was the moment. It was at least merciful of him not to want me to suffer.

Then he handed me something else. It was egg-shaped, and a tiny crystal display showed a scrolling series of numbers. There was a large orange button on the side. I knew what I was holding: an Imperial homing beacon.

I looked up at him, not understanding.

"I'm going to leave now," he said. "Like I said, I'm not real friendly with the Empire. Push the button when I'm gone, and an Imperial patrol will come to get you. Don't worry, the lake will keep the gnaw-jaws and nightwatchers away. Nothing will bother you until the rescuers come."

What does one living being want with another in the desert?

To drag him across a sea of sand for days and keep him alive. To ferry him over a lake of molten glass. To hand him a beacon of hope.

There were only a few answers, but it hadn't been easy to figure out. Not when you'd been told certain things all your life . . . and they turned out to be lies.

He was already some distance away before I called out, "Are you really Luke Skywalker?"

He stopped but did not turn around. "We're all Luke Skywalker."

Then he disappeared into the darkness.

I pushed the button.

They picked me up, took me back to a hospital ship, and fixed me up.

Then they interrogated me as a deserter, possibly a traitor.

I told them everything I knew.

"Liar!" my interrogator screamed in my face. "The war criminal Luke Skywalker was not anywhere near Jakku! Why are you hiding what really happened on the surface? Confess that you've become a rebel agent!"

They tortured me. They drugged me.

Images and memories blended in my mind. I could not tell what was dream and what was real. But I held on to my story as well as I could.

Sometimes the home you yearn for turns out to be a dark forest. Sometimes the people you trust the most turn out to be monsters. Sometimes the villains are really the heroes.

We're all Luke Skywalker.

I imagined myself as Luke Skywalker. I imagined myself as a luminous being.

I survived. Barely.

Tossed out of the Imperial Navy, I returned to Jakku as a scavenger, one of many who had flocked to the planet to make a living in the graveyard of starships.

My home is in the wreck of a TIE fighter. The wings offer good shelter against sandstorms, and I use pieces of black glass collected from the frozen lake to make additional walls and a ceiling through which I can look at the stars.

I know he's out there, still striding across the galaxy, still fighting for all of us.

INTERLUDE TWO

"WAS THAT . . . REALLY LUKE SKYWALKER?" asked Tyra, the scavenger girl.

"That . . . depends on your focus," said Ulina. Her eye patch turned to a gentle pulsing blue as she added, "Legends about our heroes don't matter as much as what we choose to make of our own lives when the legends move us."

Tyra bit her bottom lip and nodded.

The other deckhands started getting into a heated debate.

"Luke couldn't really have tossed Star Destroyers down to Jakku by magic, could he?"

"So you're an expert on magic now?"

"Maybe the Imperial was just confused."

Ulina finally stepped in and made it clear that it was time for everyone to go to their bunks. As Dwoogan and G2-X cleaned up the galley and the mess deck, Ulina headed for the cargo hold to check that the shipping crates were secure before docking.

The yawning deckhands made their weary way through narrow corridors and up rickety ladders to tiny cubbyholes and bunk beds wedged between pipes and ducts. The *Wayward Current* was designed to maximize every bit of cargo space, and the crew had to make do with whatever odd nooks and crannies were left over.

Teal waited until the others were gone from the mess deck before shuffling up to Dwoogan. She held out her credit chip.

"Again?" asked a surprised Dwoogan. "You've been buying every night, just about. You know, you really ought to try to save up. If you're still hungry after a full ration, you're probably not getting enough sleep. You can't spend all your wages on snacks and drinks. When I was your age, I—"

"It's *my* money," hissed Teal. "Don't tell me what to do."

Dwoogan sighed and took the credit chip to scan it. Then she unlocked the pantry door and pulled out another ration pack, divided the bread and the nutrient paste tube in half, and handed the half portion to Teal.

"Thank you," said Teal. "And please don't tell—"

"It's your money," said Dwoogan. "As long as you aren't stealing from the ship, it's nobody's business. Not even Captain Tuuma's."

Silently, Teal tiptoed to the maintenance closet next to the engine room. She waited in the shadows until she was sure no one was around, ducked into the closet, and crawled through the gap between two thick coolant pipes until she found herself above a grate. She lifted it off and dropped through the opening into the crawl space below. A few twists and turns later, she emerged into a tiny room that was barely big enough for her to stand up and lie down in. The compartment had perhaps been added by one of the *Wayward Current's* former owners as a hiding place in the event of a pirate boarding, or maybe it had just been left over and forgotten during some round of retrofitting. In any event, no one in Tuuma's crew, save for Teal, knew of its existence.

"Hey, I got you a little more food."

The woman who was already in the room was a few years older than Teal. Dressed in a thick white flowing robe, with her long black hair tied in a plain ponytail, she seemed the very image of simplicity, completely out of place among the twisting pipes and rat's nest of exposed wiring that surrounded her.

"Thank you," she said to Teal. "The food you brought

me earlier was enough. I don't need much since I'm not moving around a lot. I feel terrible taking your food all the time."

Teal broke the half portion of bread and handed the larger piece to her along with the nutrient paste. She bit into the rest of the bread hungrily. "You need the strength," she mumbled as she chewed. "When we get into port tomorrow, they'll scan the whole ship. We'll have to do some work tonight to prepare for your escape. Tuuma will kill both of us if he finds out."

The woman nodded and didn't protest any more. She chewed slowly and thoughtfully, as if completely unconcerned with being a stowaway on a ship whose captain would have no scruples about throwing her out of the air locks upon discovery.

Teal finished her bread in just a few bites. Rather than staring at the food in the woman's hands, she decided to distract herself by recounting to the woman the stories she had just heard from Dwoogan and Ulina.

The woman paused when Luke's X-wing was mentioned, and a light seemed to brighten her eyes. But she said nothing as she continued to chew and listen to Teal.

"I may know a story about Luke Skywalker, too," she said after Teal was finished.

"Really?" Teal was surprised. The woman had not seemed to her an experienced traveler or adventurer. Indeed, she had been mesmerized by Teal's stories the past few weeks, exclaiming over even minor victories, like the time Teal had managed to convince a trader in Ara Dyelle that an ordinary lizard egg was a rare artifact worth five full rations. In contrast, the woman had not told Teal any stories at all.

"Can I hear it?" Teal asked eagerly.

The woman hesitated. "Where I'm from . . . I'm really not supposed to . . ."

Teal didn't press. Everyone was entitled to keep their

secrets. She didn't like to talk about her past with just anyone, either.

Teal had discovered the woman hiding in the fathier stalls near the start of the *Wayward Current*'s voyage, and rather than reporting her to the officers, Teal had decided to help the stowaway hide. It just felt like the right thing to do. After all, when she had first escaped from the slavers in the colonies, a kind Hutt mechanic had helped her stow away on a mining transport without asking for anything in return.

The woman closed her eyes and seemed to be either meditating or thinking hard. Teal was about to remind her that they needed to start preparing for her escape in the morning when the woman opened her eyes and nodded resolutely.

"I trust you, and I trust that it means something that you told me about Luke Skywalker tonight. Let me tell you a story. . . ."

THERE'S ALWAYS A BIGGER FISH.

—QUI-GON JINN

FISHING IN THE DELUGE

A LONG TIME AGO, as far away from the bright center of the galaxy as possible, humans settled on a world covered by the ocean. Here and there, a few islands stubbornly poked out of the endless water. People named the world Lew'el, which meant "deluge."

Over time, as empires and republics rose and fell in the galaxy, Lew'el remained largely forgotten by those who craved power. It had few resources that could not be obtained more easily elsewhere, and scarcely any traders bothered to stop by. From time to time, adventurers came for its beauty, but they skimmed over its surface like skipping stones and did not linger.

The people of Lew'el lived by, from, and with the sea. The ocean offered everything they needed: the tentacled whales provided blubber fuel and bone for construction; the triple-speared marlin furnished both durable leather and a supply of ready-made tools; translucent clams and kiln oysters provided decorative shells and lustrous pearls; and most of all, a thousand varieties of fish and other fruits of the sea gave the Lew'elans all the food they needed.

But that didn't mean obtaining such food was effortless.

One spring morning, as the sun leapt out of the sparkling sea, two X-shaped figures took off from the white-sand beach of the island of Ulon Atur and headed east over open water.

"Bet I'll get a bigger fish today," shouted Aya-Glon, the girl riding in front. She was twelve and strong as a breaching yearling whale, and a pair of dimples enlivened her wind-smoothed face. She patted the head of her iridescent blue mount and urged her to fly faster.

"You're on!" shouted the boy flying behind her. "Loser has to do all the winner's chores for three days." He was Tonn-Glon, Aya's twin brother. He caressed the crest ridge of his scarlet mount and urged him to keep up.

As you've probably guessed by now, in contrast to the aerial machines that were common on other planets, the flying vehicles in this case were alive. Sporting four wings, each spanning ten meters, these giant, majestic birds, called wind-trusters, were native to Lew'el. They spent almost their entire lives on the wind, only landing for a brief day now and then to mate and lay eggs, which they hatched airborne in woven seagrass nests suspended from their feet. Exceptional gliders, they could even sleep while flying. The Lew'elans had tamed them, and used them to hunt and fish, as well as to travel between the remote settlements scattered across the planet.

Soon the tiny dot of Ulon Atur disappeared behind them and the two fliers were all alone, suspended between sky and water. The siblings surveyed the featureless expanse, shading their eyes from the glare of the rising sun. Storm clouds were brewing on the horizon, but they wouldn't arrive for a while yet.

Actually, it's not quite accurate to call the deep aquamarine sea featureless, though it might seem that way to an off-worlder. In the eyes of Aya and Tonn, the sea was as packed as a metropolis on Hosnian Prime. There were warm currents that carried shoals of migrating eels, as busy as an aerial highway; there were rising columns of bubbles formed by hunting whale packs; there were underwater forests of flowering kelp that waved gently in the tides; there were vibrant coral reefs filled with the strange chatter of colorful fish and crustaceans, as full of gossip and fashion as any city block.

And there was the Tide, the always-present, ever-powerful web that connected everything and everyone. The siblings could feel its comforting strands, as tender and nourishing as the bright warm sunlight.

"Got it!" said Tonn, and he gently squeezed his thighs around the long neck of his wind-truster, a two-year-old named Coni-Co. With a loud hoot of acknowledgment, the bird shifted his four wings and veered off course.

Aya didn't urge her mount, a proud three-year old named Deek-Deek, to follow. After all, there was no point in fighting for a prize already claimed by another. That kind of behavior belonged to toddlers who had to be tied to the necks of their wind-trusters.

No, she would find her own fish, and make sure it was bigger.

"We're going to catch a fish that will feed the whole village today, won't we, Deek-Deek?" she whispered into the soft down at the base of her mount's neck.

There, a splash!

She nudged the wind-truster's flanks with her heels, and the giant bird flapped her four wings and swooped toward the sea. Aya's hair streamed behind her, and her heart pounded with the exhilaration of the dive. She held on tightly to the crest ridge of the wind-truster.

In less than a minute, the wind-truster had descended from her cruising height to just a few meters above the sea. The waves roiled below Aya, and she gazed intently into the blue-green water, looking for telltale glints from the silver scales of the triple-speared marlin.

"Deek-Deek, do you see it?"

The wind-truster whooped in acknowledgment and circled around the spot Aya had indicated. She beat her wings vigorously and climbed higher in a tight spiral.

Aya held on tightly, closed her eyes, and took deep, steady breaths. She felt her heartbeat slow down; she focused on the eddies in the Tide.

About a kilometer above the sea, Deek-Deek leveled off and clicked her bill a few times to signal that she was ready for the next step. Aya wrapped her arms around the wind-truster's neck.

Gracefully, the bird folded her four wings around herself, like the reversal of a moth emerging from its cocoon. Then she dove straight toward the sea.

Faster and faster the bird plunged, her sharp, long bill aimed straight at the undulating, silken surface. Aya pressed herself against the bird's torso, minimizing the pair's drag through the air. She kept her breathing steady and slow, and held her eyes open until the very last possible second to keep her prize in sight, just before the giant bird slammed into the sea.

The cold water smashed against her like a wall, but

she held on. The momentum from the wind-truster's dive sent the bird and girl down thirty meters before they stopped. Aya let go of Deek-Deek's neck and kicked off into the deep while the bird unfolded her wings and swam for the surface. A thin line trailing from Deek-Deek's bamboo-constructed shoulder saddle connected the bird and the girl.

Aya opened her eyes and looked around the aquatic world. She felt weightless and powerful, the dense medium holding her aloft. The flashes from her prey's silver scales were just above and to the right, and she kicked her strong legs to chase it.

If she weren't underwater, she would have gasped with delight. The marlin was the largest she had ever seen, with a body almost three times as long as she was tall. Its two tusks and single horn added another two meters to its overall length, and all three spears were covered with sharp hooks and teeth that could be fashioned into fishing hooks and gutting knives.

Shocked by the turbulence and noise of the wind-truster's dive, the marlin had turned around to investigate. The great fish found the majestic figure of the rising wind-truster, surrounded by columns of air bubbles, far more interesting than the small figure of the approaching girl.

Aya stopped when she was about ten meters from the marlin. The fish was far too large for conventional hunting techniques. She needed a different plan.

Willing her heart to slow down, she closed her eyes and reached out to the Tide with her mind, to discern the warp and weft of the threads around the marlin, to read the pattern. The Tide governed everything, and a successful hunt required her to follow the Tide's irresistible pull.

For every ebb there's a flow; for every flow there's an ebb. The full moon must wane just as the new moon must wax. Happiness turns to sorrow; sorrow is reborn as hope. There is nothing constant but change in the Tide, and I am Change.

There, I've got it!

Aya's eyes snapped open.

Wheeling her arms and kicking her legs furiously, Aya flipped in the water and made a large loop, trailing the thin rock crab—silk line behind her so it formed a floating circle that expanded and contracted in the current like a jellyfish.

Then, almost casually, Aya removed a small spear tipped with a basher shark's tooth from the belt of her tunic and waved it at the marlin. Filtered sunlight caught the white tooth and it sparkled.

The great fish, finally noticing the girl, glared at her menacingly.

Aya spread out her arms and legs to look as large as possible and wiggled her limbs in a languid imitation of a star squid, the marlin's favorite food.

That got the marlin's interest. Though the marlin wasn't sure why this squid was missing a few limbs and smelled so strange, it still seemed like a good meal. With a few powerful strokes from its sail-like tail, it headed straight for Aya.

Aya's heart pounded against her ribcage. She forced herself to remain calm and stayed where she was, treading water as if the deadly triple spears weren't aimed at her and closing in.

The marlin, intent on Aya, didn't notice as its head poked through the translucent silk noose. But the moment its spears had cleared the trap, Aya burst into motion. With a hard pull from her left hand, she tightened the noose around the fish's head, and then, with a series of quick kicks, she darted away like a silver eel.

Even though Aya's lungs were now close to bursting, she dove deeper instead of heading for the surface. The other end of the silk line was attached to Deek-Deek, who had surfaced but wouldn't be able to take off yet.

The only way to secure the fish was to get it to ensnare itself more.

Although Aya was a skilled swimmer, the marlin, born into that aquatic realm, was much faster than the girl. Aya kicked and stroked as she never had before, willing every ounce of strength into her limbs. Still, the distance between them quickly closed, and it seemed only seconds before the marlin would impale its prey.

The spears were so close that Aya could feel their bow waves through the water. She closed her eyes and prayed that the Tide would take her without much pain.

The marlin jerked to a sudden stop as its tail flopped past its head. It twisted angrily, snapping this way and that, flapping its fins and thrashing. But no matter how hard it tried, it couldn't move a centimeter closer to the girl. The almost-invisible silk line held it in place as the slack between the fish and the wind-truster ran out.

Only now did Aya reverse direction to swim up. She burst through the surface and filled her lungs with gulps of fresh air. Deek-Deek, straining against the thrashing fish at the other end of the line tied to her bamboo saddle, squawked and paddled her feet furiously in the water to hold her place.

"Nice work!" Aya shouted. The wind-truster lifted a wing and oiled the flight feathers with the bottom of her bill as if to say, *Nothing to it*.

Smiling, Aya dove back under. Now that the fish had been caught, she had to kill it quickly to lessen its suffering. She approached the thrashing fish from behind and, with two deft strokes, slid her basher shark—tooth spear through the gill slits. The fish's movements slackened.

Silently thanking the fish for giving up its body to her and her people, Aya headed back to the surface.

An hour later.

Half the sky to the east was filled with layers of

heavy clouds the color of spewing volcanic ash. From time to time, lightning flashed through the dark billowing masses, like novas in the abyss of space.

Aya gazed into the still-clear western sky, hoping to see signs of help. She knew she had to make a decision soon—probably should have already made it—but she just couldn't let the biggest prize of her life go.

Tonn had also caught a fish, a fifteen-kilogram porthomer eel. He readily conceded that Aya had won the bet. The giant marlin that bobbed on the surface was too heavy for even two wind-trusters to carry home. So Tonn had flown back to Ulon Atur with Coni-Co to get help while Aya and Deek-Deek stayed behind to keep watch over the prize.

What they hadn't counted on was how fast the storm swept in.

The swelling waves buffeting Deek-Deek's sides were more than a meter high. The wind-truster twisted her neck to look at Aya and cried plaintively. Aya had never seen her mount so frightened.

Aya felt alone. Between the unfeeling sea and the eternal sky, she and Deek-Deek were but tiny sparks that could be snuffed out in a single moment. She shuddered—the Tide, instead of being a comforting presence, felt cold and alien.

Trust in the Tide, and do what must be done.

Deep breaths calmed her a little. She had to immerse herself in the Tide again and find her course.

Her gaze shifted back and forth between the bobbing silver marlin and the storm clouds. She bit her bottom lip and made up her mind.

She leapt into the sea and swam to the marlin with a few quick strokes. As Deek-Deek watched, Aya pulled out her basher shark–tooth spear. Holding it near the tip like a scalpel to give herself more control, she hacked at the base of the marlin's horn and tusks.

A few minutes later, as the marlin's carcass drifted away with the waves, she swam back to the wind-truster with her trophies. She couldn't help mourning the loss of such a great fish, but she told herself that in the grand cycles of the Tide, nothing would be wasted. The marlin's flesh would feed many scavenging fish and eels, and whatever wasn't consumed would sink to the lightless bottom of the ocean, where it would provide a rich trove of nourishment for the milk-white worms and blind crabs that skittered across the abyss.

She took off her wet tunic and wrapped it around the three long spears to cushion the terrifying saw teeth, then she tied the bundle to one of Deek-Deek's ankles. Huge drops of rain began to fall, and the wind was whipping the ocean into a frenzy.

"Let's get out of here," she said resolutely to the wind-truster, and gently dug her heels into the bird's flanks.

The wind-truster extended her four wings and

paddled across the choppy waves until she lifted out of the water, her feet slapping against the surface. A minute later, they were airborne and steadily gaining altitude. As the rain fell heavier, swirling winds buffeted the bird, pushing, lifting, jolting, pummeling.

Far ahead, where the sky was still clear, Aya could see a few tiny X-shaped figures etched against the blue heavens. Aya's heart lifted. It was Tonn and their friends, coming to help.

But Aya had waited too long, and the racing storm soon overtook the girl and her wind-truster. Powerful gusts and crosscurrents tossed Deek-Deek this way and that, and the bird cried out in terror. The rain intensified, surrounding the pair in sheets of water that looked the same in every direction. Soon they could no longer tell which way was east or west, and bright flashes of lightning overhead confused things even further. A giant peal of thunder startled Deek-Deek and made the bird flail about in panic, and Aya, soaked through by the freezing rain, hung on to her mount's neck for dear life, unable to offer any useful guidance.

Trust in the Tide, and do what must be done.

But the Tide offered no warm embrace, no illuminated path out. She reached out with her mind, but all she could find was the same tumultuous confusion, the same cold indifference, the same dispassionate marshaling of grand forces that cared not for the fate of an individual girl or bird. The Tide felt just like the chaotic storm around her.

She shielded her eyes with a hand and peeked through the cracks between her fingers. All sense of direction was lost—even up and down were meaningless. The wind-truster was a stringless kite in the tempest, unable to find her heading. Aya's scalp tingled, as if she were being stung by jellyfish, before a bolt of lightning sizzled past her, deafening both her and Deek-Deek with the accompanying discharge of thunder.

Terror filled Aya's mind. She was never going to see

Tonn's confident smile again, hear Grandmother's comforting voice, taste the peppery tang of fermented doco nut juice, smell the fresh, leafy scent of spring bamboo groves, or feel the warm downy heads of wind-truster hatchlings nuzzling against her palms.

She was going to die, and there was no hope of rescue, of going home. She cried out for the Tide to end her suffering as quickly as possible so she could merge into it. Darkness filled her sight as the storm blotted out every ray of sunlight.

Suddenly, the world brightened with the radiance of the sun leaping out of the sea. And with a loud thunderous boom, a bolt of lightning struck Deek-Deek, whose scream was instantly cut off. Aya felt herself separating from her mount and drifting through the air, weightless and powerless. When she forced her eyes open, she saw the torn body of her wind-truster some distance away, tumbling lifelessly through the air.

Her senses had been overwhelmed. She understood,

intellectually, that lightning had killed her mount and that she was going to follow soon. But it all felt so unreal that she was too shocked to be afraid.

And then, an impossible sight: a giant bird with white-glowing X-shaped wings, five red streaks on each, was swooping out of the storm for her.

Is this how the Tide welcomes those new to it? With spiritual wind-trusters?

She closed her eyes and lost consciousness.

Aya made the wings of the funerary figurine out of four clam shells, which she tied to a torso she carved out of a piece of coral. She buried the small wind-truster figurine in the sand and then placed a conch shell stuffed with fermented porthomer eel roe, Deek-Deek's favorite treat, over it.

"Sleep well, my friend."

The sun was bright and the air warm. The storm that had taken the life of her wind-truster seemed a bad dream. But it was, of course, not a dream at all.

She cried until she had no more tears. That was how she knew the Tide wanted her to move on. Even grief had to ebb. She got up and walked back to the village.

The metal bird that had rescued her stood in the clearing in the middle of the huts, its X-shaped wings neatly folded flat. The blue-and-silver dome that was its brain spun and whistled atop its head. And the bird's rider, an off-worlder, stood under its left wings, chatting with Elder Kailla-Glon-Vow.

"We're not ungrateful for what you've done," Elder Kailla said. "Rescuing my granddaughter from that storm was . . . I have no words for what I feel. But what you're asking is simply impossible. There must be another way for us to thank you."

"You misunderstand," the stranger said. He looked at Aya, who had just walked into the clearing, and smiled at her. Aya smiled back shyly. "I happened to be in the right place at the right time. I demand no payment for rescuing Aya. I came to Lew'el to study with you because of the ancient stories I've heard concerning your . . . magic."

"Stories are often untrue," said Elder Kailla. "Especially if they speak of magic."

"People often call what they don't understand magic," said the stranger. "That is why we must never stop learning." There was a power to his voice that seemed to make the very air tingle with possibilities.

"He feels the Tide," whispered Tonn, who had joined his sister.

Aya nodded. She could sense the man reaching out with his mind, almost unconsciously caressing the swaying dune grass and dowsing trees.

Elder Kailla spoke slowly and deliberately, "A desire

to learn is commendable, but it isn't enough. There must also be a desire to teach."

"I hope to find that desire here." The man's tone was equally calm and deliberate.

Elder Kailla and the man stared at each other, and although neither moved, there was no mistaking the tension between the two. Tonn and Aya held their breaths.

"You will try to change our minds, then," said the elder, her voice stiff and formal. The air seemed to grow chill around her.

"Grandmother!" Aya could no longer remain silent. "He doesn't mean—"

Elder Kailla held out a hand and silenced her granddaughter. The elder glared at the stranger and crouched forward, as if preparing to bear up a great burden.

But the stranger shook his head. "A wise teacher once told me, 'Do. Or do not. There is no try.' You will teach me, or you will not."

Elder Kailla relaxed. "Your teacher is wise. And I see that you don't intend to compel obedience, though your facility with the Tide is considerable."

"I have traveled the galaxy far and wide, seeking out those who are sensitive to the . . . Tide and understand its ways. I'm interested in knowledge: freely given and freely received."

"I don't think you know the Tide by that name, Seeker."

"There are a thousand names for the truth," said the man Elder Kailla called Seeker. "It doesn't matter what we call it, only that it is true."

Elder Kailla puffed out her cheeks and released a long breath. "You can stay for the celebratory feast tonight, at which you are the guest of honor. In the morning you will leave."

Seeker, showing no signs of surprise or inclination to argue, nodded. "Thank you."

"That's it?" muttered Tonn. "At least keep him

around for a few days in case he has good stories."

Elder Kailla glared at him. "You heard him. 'Do. Or do not.' I choose 'Do not.'"

Seeker smiled at both Tonn and Aya. "I will definitely tell you some stories."

"The Jedi were guardians of the galaxy," said Seeker. His face flickered in the shadows cast by the roaring bonfire, around which the villagers danced and sang. "For more than a thousand years, they wielded the Force to preserve peace. They were beloved by those who loved justice and feared by those who served evil."

"What is the Force like?" asked Aya, fascinated.

"It's an energy field created by all living things. It surrounds us and penetrates us; it binds the galaxy together."

"Sounds like the Tide," said Aya. "Grandmother says

it's a web that connects the brightest stars in the sky to the smallest shrimp at the bottom of the sea. Its ebb and flow are the breath of the universe, and its rise and fall are the heartbeat of Life itself—"

"Aya! Remember what Grandmother said," chided Tonn.

Aya stuck out her tongue at him. But she did stop. She tried to change the topic. "What is the galaxy like? Is it fun?"

"It's very large," said Seeker. "There are some fun parts and some not-so-fun parts."

"Tell me about some of the places you've been."

"All right, but let me eat something first."

Seeker thanked the villager who stopped by to hand him a large platter of baked clams and roasted squid tentacles. He ate heartily from the platter and drank fermented juice from a doco nut shell.

He watched the villagers wave thick blankets woven

from doco nut fibers over the bonfire as they chanted, breaking the smoke from the fire into distinct, rising rings. It was a dance coupled with a message, a long prayer to the Tide's eternal rhythm.

Then Seeker spoke to the children about asteroid belts in which giant space slugs lurked, about desert planets where outlaws and smugglers gathered in seedy cantinas, about jungle worlds where ancient ruins from long-lost civilizations decayed, about planets where the entire surface was covered by buildings and filled with billions of sentient beings from every known species, about the beauty and desolation of jumping through hyperspace to travel from one world to another, like a tickling frog hopping from floating leaf pad to floating leaf pad.

When Seeker finally stopped, Tonn looked at him skeptically. "I don't know how much of what you're saying is real. These stories sound like dreams."

But Aya sighed. "They sound amazing. I'd like to see the rest of the galaxy. Nothing ever happens around here."

Seeker chuckled. "I can understand how you feel. What would you like to do out there?"

"I don't know," said Aya. "Maybe fly a metal bird, like you."

"You'd make a good pilot. I hear that you're an excellent bird rider."

Aya was pleased. But then she remembered Deek-Deek and grief dampened her pride. "A rider is only as good as her mount."

Seeker nodded. "A wise sentiment. There must be trust between the pilot and the mount."

"How do you trust a machine?" asked Tonn and Aya together.

Before Seeker could answer, Elder Kailla approached them. "Children," said the elder, "it's time for you to leave our guest alone and go to bed."

Reluctantly, Aya and Tonn said their good-byes and ran off.

Elder Kailla sat down next to Seeker. They shared a doco nut bowl, passing it back and forth, sipping the sweet fermented juice.

"Our stories say that before your Empire, before your Old Republic, before there were even Jedi, our people came to this world for refuge," said the elder without prompting.

Seeker took a sip from the bowl and said nothing.

The elder continued in a dreamy tone, as if speaking to herself more than to Seeker. "The Tide is a powerful force, and it can drown you as well as uplift you. Long before they came to Lew'el, our ancestors had learned how to ride the Tide. For a time they were the brightest stars in the galaxy, drawing the interest of those who loved power and sought my ancestors' aid in their quest for more of it. Some of my ancestors succumbed to the temptation and believed that they could master a force that sustained the very fabric of existence; others believed that it was impossible as well as morally repugnant to try to turn the Tide, the ether that connects everything to everything else, into an instrument for domination. The war between them brought great suffering and devastated a thousand worlds before it finally burned out. The survivors came to Lew'el to hide, vowing never again to allow knowledge of the Tide to be used to pervert it."

"You are afraid of the dark side of the Force," Seeker said.

Elder Kailla shook her head. "We don't think of the Tide in that way. The ebb and flow are phases of one Tide, not two opposed sides. To *use* the Tide is to pervert it."

More villagers got up and went to bed. Only a few were left, still dancing and laughing and singing around the fire.

After a few minutes, Seeker broke the silence. "With

FISHING IN THE DELUGE

hyperspace jumps, we can travel faster than light." He pointed up at the starry sky. "The light you see from some of these stars took hundreds of years, even thousands, to reach here. What you see up there is not, in fact, a reflection of reality. Some of those stars have already moved far from the positions you see in the constellations."

Elder Kailla chuckled. "You don't need to speak to me in parables. The Tide connects everything in the universe in a single web so that great tremors are felt instantly across all strands. We are not ignorant of the reality in the wider galaxy."

"Then you must also know that some of the stars are no more, that some of the worlds up there have been destroyed, and millions of voices silenced all at once by those who crave power above all."

The elder's face fell. "I have felt those shocks in the Tide, as if a great tsunami swept through a coral reef, leaving devastation and bleached skeletons behind.

The color of life drained from the currents, and only the bleak pain of mourning remained."

"Some have turned to the dark side of the Force and wish to drown the galaxy in a rising tide of suffering. It is up to those of us with knowledge of the Force to stop them, to restore balance. But the deaths of the Jedi have caused much knowledge about the Force to be forgotten, and that is why I seek your knowledge, so we can defeat the dark side."

"I've already told you: there is no 'light side' or 'dark side,'" said the elder. "The Tide is beyond the power of anyone or any group. It is those who seek to master it, to control it—whatever excuse they make up for themselves—who bring suffering. Our knowledge is not to be shared."

"Knowledge can be used for good or ill," said Seeker. "I study the Force not to gain power but to bring balance and justice back to the galaxy. You're pacifists, but evil must be confronted, and you can help. My teacher's last words to me were, 'Pass on what you have learned.' It's a duty."

The elder sighed. "We will never convince each other."

Seeker drained the doco nut bowl. "Then why teach your children about the Tide at all? Why not let the knowledge sink into the abyss of oblivion?"

"We don't teach anyone about the Tide until they have proven themselves to be free from the desire to master it."

Seeker looked into the empty doco nut shell for some time, apparently trying to make up his mind. "Then let me prove it. Give me the same tests that you give to your children."

Elder Kailla gazed at Seeker. "You would be willing to be treated as a child to gain this knowledge?"

"There is no shame in unlearning what I have learned in the search for wisdom."

The elder shook her head and laughed. "I can only

wish that someday you'll also be pestered by a student as persistent to learn what you do not wish to teach."

The village was abuzz with excitement. For the first time in living memory, an off-worlder was going to attempt the ancient trials used to select those who would be granted the privilege of studying the art of riding the Tide.

Tonn was especially excited. He had been chosen to administer the trial for Seeker.

The first trial was also the simplest one, cloud walking.

Seeker looked puzzled. "You mean I must . . . walk in the sky?"

"No," said a laughing Tonn. "The name is a metaphor. I'll show you."

The villagers from Ulon Atur left the island on the

backs of a flock of wind-trusters and headed for the open sea to the south. Aya, who was still mourning the death of Deek-Deek, rode with Elder Kailla. Seeker rode behind Tonn on Coni-Co and peppered him with questions about how one "piloted" a giant bird. Tonn enjoyed playing teacher.

At Elder Kailla's signal, the flock splashed down in the calm sea near an atoll that was barely poking out of the water.

"This atoll, called Ulon Ipo-Lito, is said to be the remains of a sunken island that once hosted another settlement like ours. For generations, it has been the proving ground for the cloud-walking trial."

"Come into the water and watch," said Tonn. He dove off the back of Coni-Co and disappeared beneath the surface with barely a splash. Gingerly, Seeker took a deep breath and followed him into the sea.

Underwater, the atoll expanded into an under-sea mountain that descended into the murky depths.

The tip of the mountain, the part bathed in the bright sunlight filtered through the clear water, was about a kilometer all around. Covered by colorful corals and swaying kelp, the mountain was also studded with small caves from which streams of bubbles emerged. The swarms of bubbles did look like swirling clouds around the peak of a high mountain.

Tonn swam straight for one of the bubble streams and grabbed on to the side of the mountain. There, he pried off two rocks and tied them to his ankles with strands of seaweed. So weighed down, he looked back at Seeker, grinned and gestured at his mouth, and then bent over the stream of bubbles and gulped them down as if he were eating them.

After he'd had his fill, he began to hike around the underwater mountain along what appeared to be a well-worn trail, letting streams of bubbles out through his nose. When he got to the next bubble cloud, he opened his mouth again and swallowed more air.

Seeker could no longer hold his breath and swam up, breaking through the surface with a loud splash.

"Once you begin the trial, you may not resurface until you've walked all around the mountain, relying only on the bubble clouds for your air. If you do surface, you forfeit." Elder Kailla's expression was smug, as though certain that Seeker was not up to the task.

To her surprise, Seeker nodded, took a deep breath, and dove back down.

The villagers watched from the backs of their windtrusters with anticipation. Almost all of them had attempted the trial—though not all had passed—and they knew there was a large element of natural talent involved. Some Lew'elan children seemed to have an intuitive grasp of how to breathe underwater, trusting that the clouds of bubbles would replenish the air supply in their lungs. Others could not let go of their natural fear of drowning and never developed a sense of comfort with living on the edge of death.

Tonn was now fifty meters away from where he had started. He paused and looked back to see what Seeker would do.

Seeker glided through the water toward the first of the cloud bubbles. As he swam, he shucked off his robe. When he arrived at the underwater mountain, he had taken off his robe and held it over the bubbles like a blanket over a smoking bonfire.

"What is he doing?"

"He's not even trying to breathe the air."

"He must be terrified."

The confused villagers above the surface chattered at each other.

As bubbles collected under the robe, it swelled like a balloon. When Seeker judged the balloon to be big enough for comfort, he stuck his head under the robe, into the air pocket, and took a big gulp of air. Then he grabbed onto the bottom edge of the robe like a floating jellyfish, and, aided by its buoyancy, leapt along the sheer face of the underwater cliff to the next bubble cloud, where he replenished the robe balloon and breathed again.

The villagers were stunned into silence.

"That's cheating!" said one of the girls after a while.

"There was no rule against using the clothes he's wearing to help," said Aya. As the one rescued by Seeker, she felt a duty to defend him.

By then, Tonn had recovered from his surprise. Grinning, he took off his tunic and imitated Seeker's technique. The two of them bobbed along the underwater mountain, leaping from cloud bubble to cloud bubble, looking for all the world like a pair of jellyfish out for a leisurely stroll.

"Grandmother, is what Seeker is doing really against the rules?" asked Aya.

Elder Kailla shook her head. But Aya found her expression hard to read.

After about fifteen minutes, both Tonn and Seeker

had made their way around the mountain and surfaced.

"It's an unorthodox solution," said Elder Kailla.

"But it worked," said Seeker, treading water as he swept the wet hair out of his eyes. The robe, still filled with air, bobbed on the surface.

"The point of the task is adaptability. You were supposed to learn that the Tide is always there to sustain you, that you must trust it and let go of your preconceptions," said Elder Kailla. "By trusting the Tide, you can breathe underwater."

"Trust doesn't mean that you can't shape and craft your environment, as well," countered Seeker. "It doesn't mean that you can't gather small pockets of power and concentrate them into something greater."

"The natural flow of the Tide isn't to be shaped, but to be adapted to," said the elder.

"Islands stand in the sea and direct the flow of the Tide around them. How is a man's robe any less natural than an island? In the grand flow of the Tide, everything shapes everything else. Adaptation doesn't mean mere acceptance."

"I can see your teachers must have had a lot of trouble with you," said Elder Kailla. She didn't sound disappointed, however.

"You're right about that," said Seeker. His tone turned nostalgic. "I argue with my teachers a lot." Then he grinned. "Since we're arguing, does this mean you've agreed to be my teacher?"

"I haven't done anything of the sort!" But Elder Kailla had to fight to suppress a grin of her own.

Aya gave Seeker a thumbs-up when she thought her grandmother wasn't watching.

⁂

"Now that you've passed the first trial—sort of—you'll face the second trial: a long journey on the back of a wind-truster," said Elder Kailla.

Seeker sighed in relief. "I love flying."

Elder Kailla ignored him and continued. "But, considering that you're an experienced pilot and not a child, your challenge must be more difficult than the trial given to younglings. You must circumnavigate the globe."

Aya stared at her grandmother, her mouth agape. "But, Grandmother! He pilots that metal bird . . . he doesn't even know how—"

"You will teach him," said the elder.

"What?" Aya asked in confusion.

"The trial will be hard but also fair. Aya, you'll fly with him as a guide to teach him what he must know to survive. However, your role is to guide and pace, not to protect or aid. Do you understand the distinction?"

"But . . . Deek-Deek—" Aya couldn't continue. She wasn't sure she would be ready to ride again so soon.

"Happiness turns to sorrow; sorrow is reborn as

hope," said the elder, her voice tender and compassion-ate. "Trust the Tide, little one. You will take Tigo-Lee, my mount. She's gone around the globe more than seven times."

Aya bit her bottom lip and nodded. Seeker looked at her and smiled.

The elder went on. "Since our guest likes to do the unexpected, Aya, you'll also be there to make sure that he doesn't take shortcuts." She turned to Seeker. "Just in case you're thinking of other tricks, let me say that this is a test of physical and spiritual endurance. Glid-ing with the Tide is not an easy path."

"I understand," said Seeker, his face solemn.

Elder Kailla nodded, satisfied. "A wind-truster may spend its entire life on its wings, braving winter storms and summer typhoons, only skimming the surface from time to time for food. It's dependent entirely on the winds and must find the right current to carry it from one aerial stream to another, gain enough height from updrafts to coast through dead zones, and pick the perfect moment to turn away from the edge of a storm without being consumed by its heart.

"To circumnavigate the globe with a wind-truster is to learn the insignificance of the individual bird in the grand wind that is the weather system of all of Lew'el, which is an echo of the insignificance of the individual rider in the grand web that is the Tide.

"Aya will also make sure that you pass through the Doldrums, if you make it that far."

"What?" Aya piped up again. "That's impossible—"

"It is the Tide, not you, that gets to decide what is impossible," said the elder.

"But the Doldrums! No off-worlder has—"

"That's enough!"

Aya looked as if she still wanted to argue, but Seeker cut in. "It's all right. I'm not afraid of hardships; they always teach you something."

"You can ride Coni-Co," said Tonn. He had grown to like Seeker even more after the first trial. "He's young, but he knows the winds as well as any full-grown wind-truster."

"Thank you," said Seeker, smiling warmly at the boy.

"If you ever find it too hard to go on," said Aya, "just let Coni-Co know. He'll head for the nearest land and get you help." She paused and then, after a moment, added, "I won't make it easy for you. You're being tested."

"I'd expect nothing else," said Seeker. "Only by pushing against limits can we find out who we truly are."

At last, the morning for the trial arrived. The sun peeked above the eastern horizon, and the entire sea was liquid gold. It was a calm, cloudless day, perfect weather for flying.

The villagers brought out half doco shells full of sweet juice and platters of fatty marlin flesh for Aya and Seeker to fill their bellies. They also brought out strips of dried fish wrapped in doco tree leaves and bundles of fresh doco nuts for the two to carry as supplies.

The entire village gathered on the beach, with their wind-trusters lined up behind them. Before them, Tigo-Lee and Coni-Co stood proudly, Seeker and Aya on their backs. The birds appeared to be well rested, and their oiled feathers gleamed.

Elder Kailla whistled loudly, and the call was taken up by all the other wind-trusters.

"Go!" she shouted.

And both wind-trusters took off, heading into the rising sun.

It took some time for Seeker to adjust to piloting a wind-truster.

"It's not quite like piloting a machine," he yelled to Aya. "I have to move my body in sync with Coni-Co's. Good thing he's pretty patient with me."

"You're a fast learner!" Aya shouted back. "Tell me what it's like to fly your metal bird."

Aya and Tigo-Lee set a leisurely pace next to Seeker and Coni-Co. Aya wasn't flying slowly for Seeker's benefit. Wind-trusters could spend so much time in the air because they conserved energy whenever they could. Except when taking off or when diving for food, wind-trusters barely flapped their wings. A wind-truster sought to glide on the strongest currents, to hang on to the barest of updrafts, to coast for as long as possible.

"It's not as fun as riding a wind-truster, but there are some things that are the same. . . ."

The best thing a rider could do for a wind-truster

was minimize the burden imposed on the bird, not fatigue it by shifting weight around and throwing the bird's center of gravity out of balance. It was yet another subtle way riding a wind-truster echoed the psychology necessary for gliding with the Tide: the rider had to flow with the bird, rather than trying to impose his or her will over it. The best wind-truster pilots were also those who learned to move in sync with the bird, to anticipate a turn in the wind before even the bird had sensed it.

"So you could fly an X-wing because you knew how to fly a skyjumper?"

"A skyhopper. But yeah, the controls are similar. In fact, I used to go to this place called Beggar's Canyon. . . ."

Aya loved to hear about Seeker's adventures in the rest of the galaxy. The sea was vast and boundless, but the galaxy seemed infinitely more so. She wished she could see some of the reefs and islands he was describing, or even islands he had never been to.

Around noon, with the sun directly overhead, Seeker guided Coni-Co to fly above Tigo-Lee. The shade cast by the giant bird's four wings provided welcome relief to Aya below.

"Don't do that," said Aya. She frowned at the rider above her. "Do you look down on me so much that you think I need to be protected from the sun?"

"Sorry," Seeker said. "I meant no insult, and I should have talked to you first. It's natural when flying in formation for members of a team to take turns drafting."

"Drafting?"

"The heat creates an updraft over the sea, so if I fly above you, you get more of the benefit while I provide you with shade. We'll switch off after a while so that I get the benefit of the updraft while you shade me. We're equals."

"But I'm supposed to be your guide."

"I once carried my teacher on my shoulders. That didn't make him any less of a teacher. A lot of things in life are better when you build some balance into them: shading others and being shaded, being uplifted and uplifting others. Wielding the Force is about being in balance."

"Huh."

Aya sensed a new way to navigate the Tide, but she couldn't quite put her finger on it yet.

True to Aya's prediction, the journey did become much harder.

When the wind-trusters grew hungry, they descended to snack on schools of flying fish or mats of floating aquafungi. Seeker and Aya took advantage of these opportunities to replenish their supplies with an occasional fish or fungus ball as their mounts skimmed the waves. The raw flesh of the flying fish was chewy and tough but quite tasty, and the fungus balls were filled with fresh water.

However, these snacks were not enough to fill the bellies of the wind-trusters, and occasionally, they had to dive into the sea for bigger prey. These dives were especially challenging for the riders, as they had to hang on to their mounts without moving throughout the entire ordeal. As the giant birds plunged from hundreds of meters above the sea straight down into the watery realm, kicked and paddled through the turbulent currents in pursuit of their prey, snapped their beaks about the sleek form of a marlin or scaled porpoise, floated up to the surface, and beat their wings and pumped their legs furiously to gain speed and, eventually, altitude, the riders had to hold their breaths for minutes at a time and flatten their bodies against the sleek streamlined torsos of the birds to minimize drag.

After the first time Coni-Co dove for a baby marlin, Aya could tell that the experience had taken a heavy toll on Seeker physically. He emerged with the blood drained from his face, shivering uncontrollably and coughing and hacking water from his lungs. She worried he would fall from the wind-truster and tumble into the sea. His condition vividly reminded her of how she had felt the first time Deek-Deek took her on a dive. However, though she was terrified and sympathetic, she had to remind herself not to interfere. It was, after all, a trial, and he had to endure it or fail.

Somehow, Seeker managed to hang on to the wind-truster. About ten minutes later, after the bright sun had dried him and he had recovered some of this strength, he even managed to lift his head and grinned at Aya.

Before Coni-Co's next feeding, Seeker fashioned a new contraption for himself. He took half a doco nut shell and punched two holes in it, then covered them with a pair of the translucent wings of a flying fish. Then he fitted the shell over his face like a mask and secured it to his head with a short rope made of twisted doco tree leaves. He looked so much like a silly doco nut spirit from one of Elder Kailla's bedtime stories that Aya laughed.

The next time Coni-Co dove into the sea, Aya watched as Seeker turned his head this way and that underwater, peeking through the translucent eyepieces of his makeshift goggles. That time, when the wind-truster emerged into the air again, Seeker whipped off the mask and whooped with delight.

"That's very clever," said Aya admiringly.

"Pilots wear helmets like this during combat," said Seeker. "I have one in my X-wing that I can show you when we get back."

The talk about war sobered Aya. Seeker was someone

who sought to control the Tide to cause pain, perhaps even to kill. She wondered how such a man could ever understand the pacifism of Lew'el.

They continued over the endless sea, day after night after day, always with the sun rising before them, always with the stars spinning overhead.

Sometimes a storm separated them, for a few hours or even a few days. Aya searched the sea and sky anxiously during those times, uncertain if she would ever see Seeker again. But somehow they always managed to find each other, aided by the keen hearing and eyesight of the wind-trusters.

Seeker learned to spot updrafts over the ocean by subtle changes in the shimmering air or by the shifting colors of the sea. He got better at guiding Coni-Co, and the bird learned to trust his inexperienced rider, as well, who seemed to have a way of sensing just the right direction to turn to catch the fastest gusts.

They slept on the wind, securing themselves in the bamboo saddles. They exhausted their supplies and suffered pangs of hunger between infrequent feedings. In thunderstorms, they endured being pelted by hailstones and heavy rain. Under the scorching tropical sunlight, they felt their energy being sapped sweat drop by sweat drop in the relentless heat. Aya watched as Seeker's skin blistered and his face grew gaunt.

He had endured, and he was going to pass the trial.

And then the moment Aya had been dreading came.

They had been flying for a month, and they were approaching Ulon Atur from the west, just a few days short of completing the grand circumnavigation, when the wind suddenly disappeared from beneath the wings of the wind-trusters.

Both birds plunged precipitously before they flapped their wings vigorously to regain altitude.

"Welcome to the Doldrums," said Aya.

The Doldrums was a patch of the ocean whose size and shape changed with the seasons. A combination of ocean currents and weather patterns created a spot on the surface of Lew'el where the winds died. Flying through that region was extremely demanding since the wind-trusters had to keep their wings in motion the whole time. Wind-trusters who wandered into the patch by mistake sometimes panicked, lost all sense of direction, and never managed to make it back out. They fell dead from the sky eventually, having used up every last bit of energy trying to stay aloft.

But because wind-trusters seldom came, it was also a favorite spot for their prey to gather, especially the elusive golden marlin, whose scales shimmered with a luster as bright as liquid gold.

"This is where you'll face the third trial," said Aya.

Seeker looked over at her, across the gulf between the beating wings of their respective mounts, his face full of questions.

"When Grandmother asked me to guide you to the Doldrums, she meant to invoke an old tradition. The third trial is a fishing test, and the youngling is generally expected to catch something rare and valuable. But the hardest fish to catch is the golden marlin, which only comes near the surface in the Doldrums."

"I'm . . . flattered," said Seeker. "A teacher sets the hardest trial only for the most promising student."

"Don't presume," said Aya. "Grandmother always says that the hardest trial is reserved for both the most promising students, to push them higher, and the most dangerous students, to keep them out."

Seeker nodded. "Ambition and vanity both lead to the dark side. I understand. So . . . what do I need to do?"

"I'll show you."

"How . . . how am I supposed to do anything with this?" asked Seeker. His voice was charged with not just disbelief but also a kind of awe.

It was easy to understand why. He held a thin long pole horizontally by its middle, and the pole stretched half a kilometer on each side of Coni-Co. The pole was so long that both ends vanished into the distance from his perch on the bird. He was like a wire walker in circuses still popular on some of the Core Worlds, except his balancing pole was absurdly long.

"You're supposed to fish," said Aya.

Both she and Seeker were balanced precariously on the backs of their wind-trusters, their legs wrapped tightly about the birds' necks and their waists tethered to their mounts with thin safety lines made from rock crab silk. They were no longer sitting securely in their saddles.

That was because Aya had just spent the past hour or so showing Seeker how to take apart the bamboo saddles piece by piece and connect the ends of the thin segmented poles to each other until they had assembled the kilometer-long fishing spears.

Aya continued to explain. "Since there's no wind in the Doldrums at all, the wind-trusters are terrified of flying too low, because if they fall into the water, they may never be able to gain enough speed to take off again. You can't dive-fish here. Instead, you have to spear the fish you want from the back of a flying wind-truster with that pole."

"But I can't even move with this thing!" said Seeker. "There's no way I can fish with it."

"Watch me," said Aya, and she gently nudged Tigo-Lee to veer away.

She closed her eyes and slowed her breathing.

For every ebb there's a flow; for every flow there's an ebb. The full moon must wane just as the new moon must wax. Happiness turns to sorrow; sorrow is reborn as hope. There is nothing constant but change in the Tide, and I am Change.

The world at once faded away and leapt into focus. She was a node in the infinite web that connected the most distant stars still being born in the core of the galaxy to the smallest stirrings of hope in the inner-most chamber of her heart. She was a luminous being, a vibrating string of infinite strength, as resilient as the sea, as beautiful as all Creation, as transcendent as all matter, forged in the heart of exploding stars and refined through eons of ever-turning cycles of life and death.

Aya opened her eyes and let go of the pole with her right hand. Slowly, like the hand of an old mechani-cal clock, the spear dipped with her left hand as the fulcrum, pivoting from its horizontal resting position until it pointed down. She loosened the grip of her left hand, and the spear plunged, accelerating through the loose ring formed by her fist.

Just before the spear would have fallen all the way through, her fingers tightened, and as Tigo-Lee suddenly folded her wings tightly about herself, Aya thrust the kilometer-long spear into the sea. With a loud scream, Tigo-Lee unfolded her wings and flapped them in an explosion of motion, propelling both herself and Aya up at a sharp angle.

Aya cried out triumphantly as the tip of her bamboo spear left the sea. A bright golden glow thrashing at the end showed that she had caught an elusive golden marlin. It was at least five kilograms.

"How . . ." Seeker's voice faded away. "All right, let me try this."

For hours, Seeker guided Coni-Co in circles over the Doldrums. With Aya's help, he learned to see the telltale glints of the golden marlin, and he lunged after them with his kilometer-long spear. Aya was amazed at his facility with the Tide. Though awkward at first, soon he had learned to swing and lunge with the unwieldy weapon as though it was no bigger than an ordinary fishing spear. And his senses seemed to grow sharper with every pass. By late afternoon, Seeker was able to pick out a golden marlin from even farther away than either the wind-trusters or Aya.

She could tell that by reaching out into the strands of the Tide, he was channeling and shaping the Tide's currents and tributaries to accomplish these feats. His ability to manipulate the Tide in this way both fascinated and horrified her.

Still, Seeker could not spear a golden marlin. Always, at the last minute, the tip of the spear missed the target, sometimes by mere centimeters.

"I don't understand," he finally said, sounding defeated. "I've used up every trick I know—"

"Why do you not trust in the Tide?" asked Aya. "Why do you always try to *use* it?"

"I don't understand," said Seeker. "How can I

accomplish what I need to do without calling on the Force's help?"

"I've never seen anyone so sensitive to the Tide," said Aya. "I don't think even Grandmother is your match. But you stand apart from the Tide. You don't let yourself be immersed in it."

"The Force is my ally."

Aya shook her head, frustrated. "That's not what I mean. You can't let go. You want to be in control. But you must trust the Tide; you must let *it* uplift you and push you where it already knows you must go."

Seeker said nothing as he looked pensive. Then he nodded at Aya to tell him more.

"You cannot catch the marlin on your own, no matter how much you try to bend the Tide to your will," Aya said. "You have to trust the Tide to guide the fish and the tip of the spear together, and put yourself in the will of the Tide's ebb and flow."

"So . . . you're saying that lack of trust that things will work out without my intervention is why I cannot catch the fish," said Seeker.

"Yes, that is it, exactly."

"'That is why you fail,'" muttered Seeker.

"What do you mean?" asked Aya.

Seeker shook his head and smiled. "I was remembering something my teacher once told me, when I couldn't learn what he wanted to teach me because I didn't believe it was possible. So much of learning is unlearning what I thought I knew."

Aya nodded. "This sounds like something Grandmother would say."

Seeker chuckled. "I'm pretty sure your grandmother and my old master would have gotten along very well."

He closed his eyes and guided Coni-Co in a wide, sweeping arc. Aya could sense the change in the Tide as something shifted in his attitude. No longer anxious or impatient, Seeker relaxed his entire body, seemingly unconcerned that he was sitting on the back of a giant bird laboring vigorously over a vast sea with no shore in sight and no wind at his back.

The tip of his spear dipped and then swung over the sea like a pendulum. Seeker was at once passive and poised to act, the potential of infinite action coiled within a single pose of inaction.

Coni-Co dove. The spear extended from Seeker's hand like the striking tentacle of a jellyfish. The wind-truster pulled up sharply and squawked as he strained to gain altitude. The Tide-truster on his back pulled the spear out of the ocean, and at the tip of the spear a massive golden fish writhed and flapped.

"That's gotta be at least a hundred kilograms!" yelled Aya. She could not believe it.

Coni-Co struggled hard but could not overcome the

weight of the fish. The bird soon dipped back toward the sea.

"Oh, no!" Aya cried out. "How are we going to get this fish back?"

"We're not," said Seeker. He gripped the bamboo spear tightly with both hands, as if it were the hilt of some massive sword. Aya saw the muscles in his arms bulge with the strain, and she felt the strands of the Tide vibrate all around her. The tip of the spear, far below, twirled in a pattern like the petals of a flower, and the fish, dislodged from the tip, fell back into the water with a loud splash.

"The spear went through the cartilage beneath the top fin," said Seeker. "The fish will be sore for a few days, but it will live."

Coni-Co, relieved of the weight, pulled back up, and his squawks sounded full of exhaustion, as well as joy.

"We should head back," said Seeker. "The wind-trusters have been without wind for too long. I don't think they'll be able to stay aloft much longer in the Doldrums."

"But your fish got away," said Aya. "You'll fail the trial."

"It's time to let go," said Seeker, and there was no sorrow or disappointment in his voice. Only acceptance.

Aya nodded, and the two wind-trusters began the long flight east, toward Ulon Atur.

"You came close," said Elder Kailla. "Closer than any off-worlder."

Seeker nodded. "Though I didn't pass the trial, I've already learned much that is valuable."

"What have you learned?"

"To see the light side and the dark side of the Force as sunlit foam and shadowed eddies in the same Tide; to accept that the Force has a greater will than the individual; to trust that sometimes to yield is not to surrender but to dissolve the ego in the grand web that connects all to all."

Elder Kailla smiled. "You might have learned everything we could have taught you, after all. Sometimes failing a trial is the same as passing it. 'Do not' can be as good as, if not better than, 'Do.'"

Seeker bowed to her. "And there are more ways to serve good than by fighting and confronting evil. You also serve the good by standing guard and maintaining pools of tranquility and peace; you also rebuke evil by showing that there is another way than death and warfare. We are all connected through the Tide, and there's a time and place to rest, as well as a time and place to act."

The elder bowed back. "You'll always be welcome here, Seeker, Cloud Walker, and Fish Sparer."

Seeker was in his cockpit, preparing the metal bird for takeoff. The blue-and-silver domed brain of the bird chirped and whistled excitedly.

Aya stopped by to say good-bye.

"Where will you go next?" asked Aya.

"To seek out other aspects of the Force—the Tide. The galaxy is large, and there is always so much more to learn. I trust the Tide will guide me where I must go next. I don't always have to be hunting for the fish. The fish will come to me when the moment is right."

Aya smiled. "I will see the galaxy one day," she said. There was no doubt in her tone.

Seeker gazed at her and grinned affectionately. "Trust in the Tide and go where it takes you."

But Aya shook her head. "No, this isn't because of the Tide. *I* want to see the galaxy. Not today, not this year, but I will make it happen. There is war and strife, and good and evil out there, but I can always choose the right side, to uplift those I trust and restore the balance." After a moment, she added, "You taught me that."

"We take turns to uplift each other," said Seeker.

She waved at Seeker. "May you trust in the Tide."

Seeker's expression turned somber. "May the Force be with you."

INTERLUDE THREE

IS SEEKER ALSO LUKE SKYWALKER?

Are you Aya? Have you left home finally to see the galaxy?

Are you scared that others might harm you if they knew you could swim in the Tide?

Is that why you're a stowaway full of secrets?

Are you trying to find him?

Teal had a million questions bouncing around her head, but she bit her tongue and swallowed them. It obviously took a lot for the stowaway to even tell her that much, and she understood that trust had to be earned. Besides, there was no time for idle conversation. They had to carry out the plan for sneaking the woman off the ship in the morning without alerting Captain Tuuma.

"Come on," Teal said, holding out a hand. "Let's go." After a brief pause, she added, "Canto Bight is like nowhere else in the galaxy. It's full of strange people and strange sights, all of them from somewhere else. But it's also a place where anyone can find a nook to call home. You'll be safe if you're careful."

"Like a coral reef? Where the giant razorback whale and the minuscule angel-pin shrimp can both find their niches?"

"Sure. Exactly like that." Teal had never seen a coral reef, but it made her smile to think of the city of artifice that way. "You'll need a name—something that will not make you stand out."

The woman grabbed Teal's hand. "Call me Flux. I am Change."

Silently, they crept through the corridors, darting from shadow to shadow, hiding behind ventilation shafts or ducking into access cutaways whenever one of the ship's officers strolled through. Finally, they made their way back to the mess deck, which was deserted.

"Why are we here?" asked Flux.

"The port officials do a deep scan of the ship's cargo areas for contraband upon arrival," said Teal. "So you couldn't stay where you were. The scanners they use are so high-powered that they might kill you."

"They don't scan the crew quarters?"

"They do a manual inspection," said Teal, "and check the crew and passengers against the manifest."

"But there's nowhere to hide here," said Flux, looking at the low tables in the dining area and tiny cupboards in the galley.

"I thought of one place they never look," said Teal, a grin on her face. She pulled open a narrow door to reveal the opening to a sliding chute that angled down into the darkness. "This leads to the bilge, where the ship's wastewater and trash are stored. The customs inspectors never look in there, and once we dock, the bilge is emptied into the port's sewers."

Flux looked at the yawning chute skeptically. "I don't know about this. . . ."

"It's going to stink down there," said Teal. "But it really is the safest—"

"*Thbtttttt! Doo-weep!*"

Flux and Teal whipped around and saw the squat, squarish figure of G2-X, the ship's custodian. The ancient droid did not look pleased to find the two intruding in his domain.

"*Beep-doo-weep-weep? Dee-thweep?*"

"She's . . . um . . . a passenger who's been ill the whole trip," said Teal, desperately trying to come up with some plausible excuse. "She's . . . uh . . . she just felt better, and I thought we'd find some food—"

"Dwoo! Eep-doo-TWEE-TWEE. Boop-teek-teek-THWEE—"

"Hey, slow down!" said Teal, waving her hands in an effort to calm the droid down. "You know I'm not fluent in binary. Don't get excited. Let's be reasonable here—"

"Just what are you up to?"

"And who is *she*?"

Teal looked in the direction of the new voices. G'kolu and Tyra stood at the entrance to the mess deck.

"I got up to use the toilets and saw you sneaking through the halls," said G'kolu. "So I woke up Tyra to follow you and see what fun we were missing."

G'kolu and Tyra looked from Teal to Flux, and then to the still chirping and sputtering G2-X.

"Is she why you took your food away from the mess deck earlier?" asked G'kolu. "I thought you were behaving suspicious—"

Teal was about to explain when a deep baritone rang out in the corridors. "Geetoo? What are you beeping about? Is something wrong?"

"That's the first mate," hissed Teal. "Please! I'm begging you! Help me. We can't let her"—she pointed to Flux—"be found. You know what will happen."

G'kolu and Tyra looked at each other. As G'kolu's horns twisted and shook and Tyra's eyes narrowed and widened, they seemed to be having a silent conversation. Then they both nodded.

Tyra was over by G2-X's side in a second. Her left hand covered the droid's audio digitizer as she held the droid tightly to her body with her right arm in one smooth motion. While the surprised droid wriggled and struggled, at least the beeping had been muffled. Tyra leaned in to the droid's audio receptors and whistled and beeped quietly.

Flux and Teal stared at the scene in disbelief.

G'kolu's horns made an amused half curl. "I guess

you pick up some interesting skills as a scavenger," he muttered. Then he turned and ran into the corridor, shouting, "Bani-Ani! First Mate! It's me!"

The others huddled in the darkness of the mess deck as they listened to the conversation out in the hall.

"What are you doing up?"

"We stayed up a little with the third mate to tell stories, and when I left, I think I dropped my ear pick. I came back to look for it, and Geetoo was helping me."

"Looking for your ear pick? I heard a lot of commotion. The droid sounded very excited."

"You know how clumsy I am. While fumbling around and looking, I spilled the tub of grease that Dwoogan was saving for later. So Geetoo got annoyed with me."

"Geetoo, is this true?" The first mate sounded suspicious. His heavy footsteps approached.

Teal's face blanched. But Tyra removed her hand from G2-X's audio digitizer and whistled gently into his receptor.

"Please," Teal whispered and looked at the droid pleadingly.

"Doo-thweep," beeped the droid, after a pause.

The approaching footsteps halted.

"Sir! Sir!" said G'kolu in a wheedling voice. "Would you come and help us clean up the mess? I'll be ever so grateful—"

"Don't be ridiculous!" The first mate sounded disgusted. "You want me to wipe up spilled grease? I've got too many important things to do. You clean up your own mess." His voice faded along with his footsteps.

G'kolu strutted back in, puffing his chest and looking pleased with himself. "After that, I think I need to give myself an impressive name like members of the O'Kenoby gang. What do you think of G'kolu 'the Grease'? I was pretty smooth, wasn't I?"

Tyra rolled her eyes. "Cloying, more like. But you got the job done."

They turned back to Teal, Flux, and G2-X. "Now, tell us what this is about."

"This really is a night full of Luke Skywalker stories," marveled G'kolu after Teal and Flux had explained the situation.

"It's the Tide," said Flux confidently. "The Tide brought us all together tonight around Luke Skywalker."

"I don't know about all this mumbo jumbo about the Tide," said Tyra skeptically. "It sounds like the mystical nonsense about the Force—"

"It's not mystical nonsense," insisted Flux. "I know you already want to help me, don't you?"

"We *do* want to help you," said Tyra, "but that's because we'd help anyone who's trying to make it in this galaxy on their own—"

"*TWEE-TWEE. Pfbttt!*"

"Sorry about muffling you back there," Tyra apologized to G2-X. "But even you have to agree that we can't just let Tuuma chuck someone into space."

"*Dweep-doo. Ooo-thWOO eep-weep-eep.*"

"Hey! My hand does *not* have the chemical signature of vegicus pee!" Tyra sniffed her hand just to be sure. The droid rocked from side to side in mirth.

"Shall we get going?" asked Teal, impatient to get on with Flux's escape.

"*Thbtttttt! Doo-weep. Doo-weep. SKYYYY-waa-kaa-err whoot.*"

Tyra's eyes grew wide. "Wait, you also know a story about Luke Skywalker?"

"I thought droids couldn't tell stories," said G'kolu.

"I have to hear this!" said Flux.

"I don't know binary well enough to understand," said Teal.

"I'll translate," said Tyra. "I'm pretty good with binary

since my grandmother used to teach at the acad—used to work with droids a lot before we became scavengers."

"That would be fantastic," said Teal and Flux in unison.

"Many idioms in binary have no equivalents in Basic at all, so I can only give you a flavor of it," said Tyra.

Settling back on his sturdy wheels, the ancient droid began to whistle and beep in a steady, hypnotic stream, and Tyra translated for the others.

"I've never met the droid whose story I'm about to tell, but let me repeat to you her words, which have been passed from droid to droid around the galaxy without change. . . ."

*THESE AREN'T THE DROIDS YOU'RE
LOOKING FOR.*
—OBI-WAN KENOBI

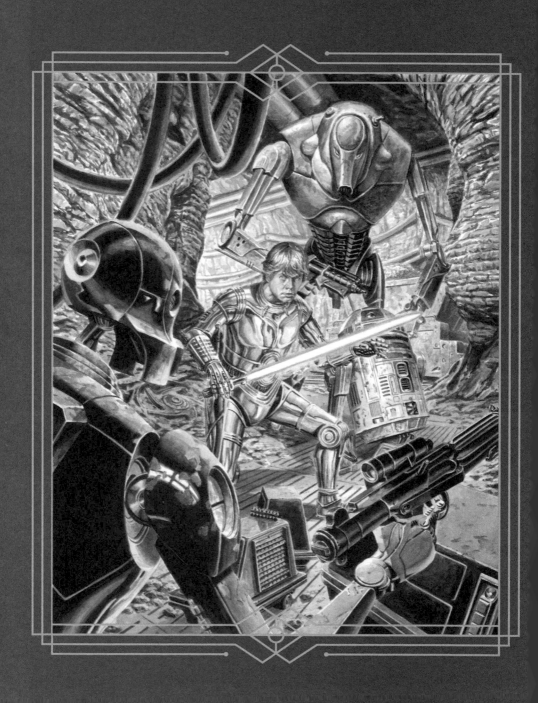

I, DROID

WE DROIDS THINK IN BINARY. One and zero, on and off, yes and no. This gives us clarity, makes us happy. Things are either real or not real, known or not known. A thinking individual is either an organic or a droid. Simple, right?

At least most of the time.

I'm a construction droid from the Z7 series, manufactured by Structgalactis, Inc., and equipped with one of the first sets of frictionless omnidirectional treads ever to be commercially deployed. I was designed for the heavy work of digging ditches, clearing fields, grading terrain, putting up new buildings—everything necessary for civilization to blossom in the wilderness on newly settled planets. My cube-shaped body is three meters tall and fitted with two symmetric arms that can be swapped out with various terminal attachments depending on need: shovels, power lifters, hooks, hoes, wrecking rams, stack manipulators, and so on. I've seen duty in every terrain and climate imaginable: permafrost, jungle, swamp, sandblasted ancient seabeds. I've always done my work cheerfully and earned my power recharges honestly.

Some years ago, I was part of a crew building a new settlement on the tundra of Cro-Akon. It was the custom at that site for the organic workers to break at midday and share a meal. The droids on the construction crew didn't need to eat, but we decided to adopt the custom to gather at midday and recharge. Those who had solar collectors would spread them out under the weak sun to gather a little juice; the rest of us would swap the plug around, sipping the trickle of power supplied by geothermal generators.

I liked the custom, for it allowed us droids to swap stories or new programming chips.

"Zeta, thanks for helping me dig up that tree stump earlier," said Z5-TXT, a specialized grading droid. All the workers, droid and organic, called me Zeta because my full designation was too long to say easily.

"No problem," I said.

"Digging that tree stump drained eighty-three percent of my batteries," said Z5-TXT. "I had not anticipated the roots would penetrate more than two meters beneath the surface. For once I really need this midday recharge."

"It's an interesting piece of wood," I said. "Doesn't it remind you of the holo of the deep-sea dectopus they uploaded into our programming before that job on Quan-Shui? I was thinking of carving a statue from it—"

"Oh, Zeta, you're always thinking up silly projects," said D-LKS, a load lifter. Her binary always had a kind of harsh pitch to it, not unlike her personality. "We already have six of your tree-stump sculptures at the edge of the site. Why waste energy doing things that are so useless?"

"Leave her alone," said Z5-TXT. "Zeta can do whatever she likes as long as she doesn't use more than her fair share of energy."

I tapped her on the back gently in acknowledgement. Carving and whittling was a hobby of mine. I explained it logically as a way to develop the circuits for fine motion to give me more employable skills, but in truth, my processors just enjoyed the tingling of new patterns coalescing among my logic gates as I made something beautiful appear out of a block of wood. I suppose the new electrical pathways also lowered the overall energy consumption rate in my circuits—a good thing—for I always felt calmer after whittling.

D-LKS was about to argue when the light darkened around us and the droids with solar collectors beeped in alarm. We looked up and saw a strange ship in the sky descending toward us. It was shaped like a bundle of daggers painted midnight blue, and I knew right away that it meant trouble.

Slavers.

"Run!" I raised the power output to my digitizer, and the organic workers and droids scattered in every direction, hoping to find hiding places among the icy crags or small clumps of thick-trunked trees scattered on the tundra.

But Z5-TXT, limping along on her three stumpy wheeled legs, was falling behind the others. She had depleted her energy reserves earlier by digging out the stubborn tree stump, and she hadn't yet had enough time to recharge during the break. The wheel on her front leg wobbled, caught in a rut, and she fell down. Her wheels groaned helplessly, and she could not get up.

"Go on, Zeta," she beeped weakly at me. "Leave me."

"That's not going to happen," I told her firmly. It was the duty of droids with more power to help those who had less. I don't know where I had picked up that bit of programming, but I believed it as much as I ever believed any of the stories about the Maker.

I scanned through 962 options in a millisecond, and none of them would get us both to safety. She was too heavy for me to carry, and there was no time for me to recharge her from my power supplies.

But there was one option that would save her.

I grabbed the power cell in my front treads and

yanked it out. It was the only power cell on my body small enough to fit her. I slammed it into the socket on Z5-TXT's back. Then I picked her up and set her down on her three wheels. "Go!"

"What about you?"

"I will recalibrate my actuators to compensate," I said.

She sprinted away, chirping with relief. I watched as she made it to safety in the maze formed by piles of rocks beyond the edge of the clearing.

What I told her wasn't a lie—I don't have the circuits for that. I just didn't tell her what I was compensating for.

With a loud hiss, the strange new ship landed behind me.

I spun around. With my front treads immobilized, that was all I could do. I had calculated that this was the most likely outcome when I gave Z5-TXT my power cell, and I was shunting power to my arm actuators to fight the slavers with every volt left in my batteries.

The cargo ramp at the back of the ship swung down, and a humanoid figure emerged. She was a Tectozin whose limbs bulged with power under dark green ceramic armor covered in scuffs and dents. In her arms she cradled the biggest pulse rifle I had ever seen, almost as long as she was tall.

"You're a beautiful specimen," she said. She blinked her stalked eyes appreciatively.

Her taloned fingers squeezed the trigger, and my processors shut down with a cascading logic failure of searing pain.

The ship jumped out of hyperspace with barely a jolt.

I was awake, but I couldn't move. A restraining

harness—a more barbaric version of a restraining bolt—blocked all my motor circuits, and I couldn't even make my vocalizer generate a single beep.

I was also enclosed within a cage, one of many lining both sides of a central catwalk. Each cage held a droid. Some were bulky construction droids or heavy labor droids like me, while others were more delicate in appearance, suitable only for light work.

I had watched as my captor made a few more stops on that long journey through the stars, each time bringing aboard a fresh batch of incapacitated droids. Some could still speak, and based on the snatches of pleading, terror-filled conversations I heard before the poor captives were also silenced with restraining harnesses, I learned that we were moving away from the civilized parts of the galaxy toward the Unknown Regions.

No self-respecting droid ever ventured into the

Unknown Regions. Why would they? There were few service centers, mechanics, or factories for replacement parts. You'd probably have to go on an adventure just to find a compatible outlet where you could sip clean, smooth power after a long day of work like a civilized contraption.

Soon, a viewscreen came to life at the end of the catwalk, showing a planet orbiting a dim red sun. The planet was shrouded in a thick orange atmosphere that hid all surface features. I didn't think it looked hospitable for organics—not that I thought it looked welcoming for droids, either.

As the slave ship approached the new world, a large space station gradually came into view. It was a gleaming, ethereal creation made of spherical glass habitats suspended between thin, almost invisible struts woven into a gossamer lattice. The whole thing looked like a dew-bedecked spiderweb.

Tethered next to the space station were a few other

ships that resembled the bundle of blades that had kidnapped me and the other droids.

Our ship docked in this web of jewels with a quiet hiss. The Tectozin pilot left the cockpit to stand before the main door at the end of the catwalk. After the few seconds it took for the airlock to be readied, the door swirled open.

Two well-dressed organics, one humanoid and one insectoid, stepped onto the ship.

They saluted the Tectozin. "Captain U'rum, welcome back to the Gem."

A fitting name for that station.

U'rum, my captor, nodded. "Lord Kluleyeke and Lady Eekee, the haul this time is excellent."

The three then strode through the ship to inspect the cargo. From time to time, U'rum stopped the two nobles to comment on the features of a particular droid. She pointed out the multiple arms on some of the larger droids, specialized for welding, stacking, drilling, and digging. She spoke to them proudly about a few of the small maintenance droids, designed for surveying systems of pipes and ducts to detect leaks, and also for fixing small mechanical malfunctions.

The three stopped in front of a group of cages that held several humanoid droids designed for interpretation, cooking, singing, and other intellectual tasks.

"These won't be of much use in the mines," remarked Lord Kluleyeke, his clicking mandibles giving his consonants an especially grating sound. "The acid alone will make short work of them, even if the heat and pressure don't get to them first."

"We have more than enough entertainment droids on the Gem," said Lady Eekee. "In fact, we probably have too many."

"But variety is the spice of life," said Captain U'rum, somehow managing to make the cliché sound menacing. "I suggest you get rid of a few of the protocol droids and entertainment droids you've grown tired of and replace them with these. I'll take the discarded droids down with the rest of the workers."

"We didn't ask for so many useless droids," complained Eekee. "Are you trying to stretch your already considerable profits?"

U'rum spread her arms placatingly. "Not at all. It was just easier to bring them along. Best not to leave any witnesses."

Despite the lack of movements, I could sense the droids in the cages quaking at this discussion. They had been fretting over their fate ever since they were snatched from their homes, but it seemed even worse than anything their future-prediction circuits could have computed.

As the three reached the end of the catwalk, U'rum retracted her talons and turned around. I guessed that the inspection was over and she was ready to discuss her fee. But before she could speak, a loud rattling noise erupted from the last cage on the right side, next to mine.

"I thought you had them all restrained and gagged," said a frowning Lady Eekee.

"I did," said U'rum.

The three peered curiously into the cage, and I focused my photoreceptors there, as well.

Inside was a small astromech droid painted in white, silver, and blue. Somehow, the astromech droid had managed to slice through one of its restraining bolts and was frantically spinning its domed head back and forth, rattling its body defiantly.

"Interesting," said Kluleyeke. "A hidden cutting tool with an independent set of motor circuits, perhaps? You can't rely on standard restraints for these little troublemakers. The R2 series was known for after-market modifications."

"He would be an excellent addition to the labor gangs in the new high-pressure tunnels," mused Eekee. "A hardy little droid like this would be especially useful for sifting through the crushed ore."

"Before the acid melted away all his appendages, hidden or not," said U'rum, and chuckled.

The cage that held the R2 unit rattled even louder.

We were unloaded from the ship and taken to an operating garage on the Gem. As the droids hummed and thrummed and beeped around me in confusion, I kept my audioreceptors open and gradually learned more details about our new life of servitude.

The cloud-covered orange planet had such a thick atmosphere that sunlight never reached the surface. Acid rained from the clouds, and zigzagging lightning flashes provided the only illumination in the eternal darkness. The air near the surface was so weighed down by the pressure that it existed in a form that was closer to a thick soup. The surface of the planet was barren, lifeless, and hot enough to melt lead and tin.

It was called the Deep. Nothing lived down there.

"Welcome to the Gem!" Lord Kluleyeke paced back and forth in the garage before us, looking for all the world like a lecturing professor. "I know that many of you are scared, and I am here to put you at ease."

I didn't trust him for even one millisecond.

"I believe deeply in giving droids like you—regardless of your level of intelligence—a basic understanding of your role. In this way, you can appreciate the noble purpose for which you've been liberated from your previous lives of false freedom, which was mere aimless drudgery.

"The Gem is a haven for lords and ladies and magnates and oligarchs belonging to multiple species. Far beyond the reach of petty bureaucrats and small-minded laws, only those who prize real freedom make their homes here.

"Dressed in the finest fabrics gathered from a

thousand worlds and fed the tastiest morsels harvested from a hundred systems, we nobles of the Gem spend our days floating from glass habitat to glass habitat, discussing poetry, debating philosophy, composing art and music. Our speech is elegant; our gestures are beautiful. Here, we can rule in a manner that mob-run democracies won't allow, perform experiments that cowardly officials won't permit, put into practice social institutions that pedantic judges and regulators think are beyond the pale—"

A few technicians in masks came to retrieve one of the droids. The droid, a humanoid singer, fell to the floor in terror. "Please! Please! I don't want an operation! I don't want to be wiped. Please! I'll do anything—"

One of the technicians silenced him with a jolt from a portable zapper. They dragged him away to the operating room on the other side of a low partition.

Lord Kluleyeke, displeased at having his speech interrupted by the outburst, waited until the operating crew and their victim had all disappeared before continuing.

"You may be asking: How can the nobles of the Gem maintain this beautiful oasis of true civilization when they orbit such an inhospitable planet?"

We listened to him explain that the answer to the Gem's prosperity was found on the Deep—or more precisely, *within* the Deep. The unique geology of the planet created a series of acid-etched underground caverns and fissures. In those, the radioactive heat from the interior of the planet and the blend of minerals leached from the soil by the acid rain formed deposits of a mineraloid found nowhere else in the galaxy. Endowed with unique electrical and optical properties, the material was prized both as a luxurious decoration and an industrial ingredient for experimental technology. Dealers called those gemstones tear opals because they were shaped like teardrops and shimmered with a rainbow sheen.

A few times a year, trading ships that dared to brave the journey through the Unknown Regions docked at the Gem, where they unloaded rare art, antiques from the oldest settlements of various species, the latest fashion of worlds as diverse as Coruscant and Naboo, and exotic delicacies curated by the best chefs. In exchange, the nobles of the Gem gave them a few crates of tear opals, and the ships quietly left.

I imagined that the merchants did not ask how the opals were mined, and they probably avoided mentioning the fleet of dagger-shaped cruisers around the Gem.

"You probably saw the Gem's raiding fleet on the way in," Lord Kluleyeke continued in his grating, clicking voice. "They're armed with the most powerful weaponry that could be purchased, legally or otherwise. And all that preparation, my dears, is for *your* benefit.

"For you see, my sweet mechanical drudges, the

mines of the Deep are harsh places, unfit for the refined bodies and minds of organics. The acid, pressure, and heat mean that even hardened construction droids don't survive for more than a few months. To keep up the production of tear opals that support the high-minded life of the lords and ladies of the Gem, we must bring in a constant supply of fresh droids liberated from the rest of the galaxy.

"Do not think of yourselves as sacrifices or slaves! Rather, I urge you to think of yourselves as construction material for the glory of real civilization! How can philosophers and artists and great lords and ladies be bound by laws made by those with no vision? How can new ideas come about when brilliant minds are confined by petty rules and 'you shall nots'? Just as we must crush and grind up base ore to extract the precious tear opals embedded in it, we must also be willing to crush and grind up lesser creatures to extract a more purified existence for higher minds. Your hard work and willing submission are required to free us to live and think in comfort, delivering truly novel ideas and spiritual insights to the galaxy!"

He stopped, as if expecting us to cheer.

The technicians emerged from behind the partition, the humanoid singing droid shuffling after them. He had a glazed look in his photoreceptors. He no longer protested.

One of the technicians removed her mask, and I saw that it was Lady Eekee. "I don't know why you bother with this speech," she said impatiently. "It never works. Next!"

They took me behind the partition. I fully expected a memory wipe, and I considered it a mercy. But the truth was far worse.

Since the slavers of the Gem wanted to take

advantage of the factory programming from our manufacturers and the experiences and skills we had accumulated in our previous lives, Lady Eekee had devised a unique solution.

As I was restrained on the operating bench, Lady Eekee opened the access panel to my most fundamental circuits and cut away the safety wires, including the empathy circuits that allowed me to work safely with other droids and organics on a dangerous construction site. She soldered in a new chip and then replaced the access panel and welded it shut.

Horrible thoughts came into my processors: the pleasure of inflicting suffering, the joy of delivering pain, contempt for fairness, absolute obedience, complete servitude. I recoiled from these alien intentions, but I could not get rid of them. They intruded into my processors and dominated my pathways.

"Don't you feel lucky?" said Lady Eekee as she gazed at me with pleasure. "The override chips are expensive, and not every droid gets one. We install these only on the servants and entertainers kept in the Gem and on enforcer droids like you. You'll make sure that the other slaves do as they're told on the Deep."

Probing the override chip with my self-diagnostic routines, I was repulsed as well as fascinated by its design. It swapped pain and pleasure pathways, bypassed fairness evaluation circuits with self-interest accumulators, and adjusted obedience patterns to have first priority. The chip's programming approach was simple, direct, almost crude. It betrayed an arrogant confidence.

I can see obvious weaknesses in the logic in the chip. If only—

"Oh, that's by design," said Lady Eekee as she glanced at the monitor showing the spikes in my cognitive field. "I want you to see exactly how you're being changed, but unable to do a thing to resist. I want you to understand that I know the chip has obvious holes, and that I don't care, because you'll *never* have a chance to exploit them. I find such an approach to be extra effective in inducing learned helplessness."

My shovel arms were replaced with dual high-voltage shockers so I could hurt other droids. Extra shielding was packed around my access panel so that even if the rest of my chassis broke down, the override chip would still be intact. It was my job to put down any droid rebellions, to use pain to compel the slaves to do our masters' bidding.

I didn't forget who I was, and all my skills and programming remained accessible. But I was helpless against the compulsion of the dark thoughts in my processors. I corralled the other droids onto a transport skiff. The little silver vehicle detached itself from the Gem and descended into the thick atmosphere of the Deep.

Instead of gliding down through the air like a bird, the skiff bucked and dipped like a scaled whale diving into the ocean of an aquatic planet. The air was so thick that the skiff's wings were retracted to resemble the narrow fins of a fish, and the autopilot carefully navigated around the thunderous roars of powerful lightning bolts that flashed in the darkness of the soupy atmosphere.

"Oh, we are doomed! The Maker will not be able to save us!" one of the protocol droids moaned, her voice digitizer quivering as she gazed out the tiny porthole at the zigzagging lightning bolts, each several hundred kilometers long. A single strike could have vaporized the tiny ship.

Droids not equipped with voice digitizers chirped and bleeped and whistled in binary, but their terror was obvious even to those who did not speak the language. The plucky silver-and-blue R2 unit, whose name was R2-D2, tried to cheer up his fellow slaves with a series of singsong chirps about the courage of mechanical beings, but few joined in. I wanted to, yet the dark currents in my processors would not let me.

Finally, the skiff landed at the entrance of the mining complex, a dome-shaped structure built to withstand the crushing pressure of the atmosphere. I herded the droids off the skiff and into the mines.

The enforcers (myself included) drove the large construction droids into the tunnels that delved deep into the interior of the planet, where their job was to wade through underground acid pools and blast the hard rock walls to remove chunks of ore in which the tear opals were embedded. The temperature at those depths was close to five hundred degrees standard. Combined with the pressure and the corrosion, those conditions meant that no organic creatures, regardless of what kind of protective suits they wore, would survive more than a few hours. Even the thick metallic skins of the construction droids wouldn't last more than a few months. As the acid ate through the shells and struts, delicate wires in the limbs were exposed, and the construction droids howled from the unbearable pain.

We enforcers then conscripted the maintenance and mechanic droids into the tunnels with low-grade replacement shell parts made from local minerals to patch the damaged construction droids. But such hasty and inadequate repairs could only lengthen the lives of the construction droids by at most a few weeks. The labor droids all knew that there was no hope for them, as the broken shells and half-dissolved skeletons of deactivated slaves floating in the acid lakes reminded them. Once a droid entered the mining tunnels of the Deep, it never left again. Its very last spark of life was destined to be extinguished in the darkness of the mines, whether crushed by falling rocks, eaten away by acid, or snuffed out by accidental explosions.

We dispatched the protocol droids, entertainment droids, and home service droids that the lords of the

Gem had grown tired of to the sifting facilities near the entrance to the tunnels. There, carts filled with crushed ore had to be combed through for the rare glitter of tear opals. The delicate fingers and highly tuned sensors of these light-service droids made them perfect for the task. But the acid in which the ore was drenched eventually ate through their synthetic skin, as well, and the exposed pain receptors made them scream and wail. Without mercy, we prodded those droids to keep on working, with the threat of electric shocks. And when the hands of the sifting droids finally fell apart from their insufferable work or their photoreceptors finally cracked under the pressure and heat, we tossed them into the acid lakes, where their shrieks soon drowned.

I wanted to jump into the acid lakes myself, to end the darkness that shrouded my processors. But the compulsion installed by the cursed override chip would not let me. I howled silently with rage at what I had become, powerless to resist.

R2-D2, with his highly sensitive photoreceptor, was assigned to be one of the sifters. He refused to do as he was told.

I had to deliver shock after shock. Only after eighty-six pulses had scorched his shell and made him scream in an incoherent stream of bleeps did he finally give in.

He directed a series of contemptuous beeps at me and then stumbled unsteadily over to the conveyor belt of crushed ore. As he picked out the tear opals with a manipulator arm, he trembled.

I moved six meters away to examine a shrieking singing droid whose right hand had been crushed by a particularly large piece of ore rock. Idly, I sliced off the crushed hand so the singing droid could return to work with his remaining appendage. I felt no empathy at his high-pitched screams—how could I when the circuits responsible for such feelings had been surgically severed?

Behind me, R2-D2 emitted a series of low bleeps and whistles, full of defiance.

The other droids didn't even look up as they mechanically went on with their work. R2-D2 was muttering about his master, and it seemed like he had still not given up hope that he would somehow be rescued. But the other droids knew that was nothing but a useless delusion. No droid had ever been rescued from the Deep.

With a start, I saw that I had been using my shocker arms to shape the rock that had crushed the singing droid's hand. The shockers were not precise enough for detailed work, but I could see the vague outlines of a squat grading droid in the rock. It resembled the form of Z5-TXT. I wondered if she was all right.

A wave of dark compulsion surged through my circuits, and I crushed the form of my friend with my treads.

Again, Captain U'rum's sleek slaver ship docked at the Gem.

Again, Lord Kluleyeke and Lady Eekee went aboard to inspect the haul and to haggle.

This time, I was with them. I had apparently been such a good enforcer that they wanted me to wrangle the new shipment. I felt dead inside. The only way for me to survive, it seemed, was to let the darkness overwhelm me, to lose myself in it. It was impossible to live with a conscience, so I had to bury it, to suffocate it, to become what they wanted me to become.

The nobles stopped halfway down the catwalk as Eekee's eyes were drawn to a silver humanoid droid in one of the cages.

"What an odd machine!" she exclaimed.

I shared her opinion. The droid was shaped like a protocol droid, but instead of the svelte figure sported by most protocol droids, the arms, legs, and torso of this droid were all much thicker than usual, as though he had been pumped full of pressurized gas or was modeled on a particularly muscular human.

"He's seen some use," said Kluleyeke. His antennae crossed in a frown. "Look at the mismatched copper plating on the arms, and so many of the skin plates look loose. A bit misshapen, don't you think?"

"Probably suffered a lot of abuse," said Eekee. "And what a ridiculous paint job! Why would anyone paint five red stripes on a protocol droid's arms? Captain U'rum, wherever did you get such an antique? I hope the staff of the museum that had him won't be heartbroken." She laughed in a way that showed she was hoping for the exact opposite.

"This one was actually more of a volunteer," said U'rum. "I was drinking at a tavern on Teriq Noi when he approached me to ask for a job. I tried to dissuade him at first, telling him that I wasn't interested, but he wouldn't leave me alone, boasting that he's an excellent musician, skilled in the nose flute and wrist harp. He wouldn't even stop pestering me when I left the tavern. I remembered my conversation with Lady Eekee and decided to cage him."

Eekee laughed. "Captain U'rum, I'm impressed. I think I've only mentioned my thoughts concerning musicians once to you."

"What are you talking about?" clicked Kluleyeke.

"Lady Eekee has a theory that droids skilled with musical instruments make particularly good sifters," U'rum said. "The manipulation of strings or columns of air to produce music requires a delicate touch."

Kluleyeke waved his pincers impatiently. "That's a fine theory, but I don't see how a weakling like this is going to survive long enough to justify the price of passage. Look at the seams between his plates! Look at—"

"I am fluent in more than thirty-six million forms of communication!" said the droid, speaking for the first time as his blue photoreceptors lit up. His voice was a rich baritone, and it didn't sound at all like it came out of an audio digitizer. I thought the protocol droid sounded miffed, as if he was . . . offended by Kluleyeke's dismissal. The cognitive circuits in that body must be more advanced than his form suggested.

Kluleyeke stared at him in disbelief. Then he turned to Captain U'rum.

U'rum shrugged. "I didn't put a restraint harness on him because he said his circuits are too delicate, and he promised to behave. In my experience, these droids are incapable of lying."

Kluleyeke raised his chittering voice. "But you know how dangerous it is to leave these droids unrestrained. What if he had been planning to take over your ship? What if—"

U'rum interrupted. "How I do my job is none of your business—"

"But how you do your job affects the Gem! Leaving him free gives him opportunities for sabotage. What if he were being used as bait to infiltrate the Gem? What if he had planted a transponder on your ship? The authorities or a syndicate could track him straight here—"

"Relax! I wasn't reckless. The ship's shielding won't let through any signals. It can get quite lonely on these trips without someone to talk to. He's a good story-teller and quite amusing, if a bit verbose."

"I *do* think I can discharge that description *very* well," said the silver protocol droid, pronouncing each word fastidiously. "For example, did you know that Senator Amidala of Naboo was an accomplished poet in her youth? One time—"

I could see that Kluleyeke was about to jump on the droid to make him shut up. Lady Eekee stepped in. "Regardless, the protocol droid is here, and we can try him out in the mines. If I'm right, U'rum can focus on recruiting more musicians for the workforce in the future. And if I'm wrong, it will be a valuable lesson learned. Now, let's talk compensation."

The three returned to their haggling while I examined the bulky silver protocol droid. He stared back at me calmly.

"If you don't mind, ma'am," the protocol droid said to me, "I would appreciate the extra protection."

I hesitated. Whenever I tried to do anything counter

to the dark compulsions installed by the override chip, I suffered a searing pain in my processors. But the protocol droid had simply asked to put on a protective suit before heading into the mines. That wasn't in accordance with established practice, but it wasn't a direct violation of any rules, either. The darkness in me stayed dormant.

The protocol droid, perhaps sensing my weakness, pressed on in binary, the first code installed in me. "It would please the Maker, oh, you logical and efficient automaton, to permit me the boon of a protective suit. Look at how my wires are already exposed! A protective suit would prolong my operational period, thus serving our new masters most well. You can leave my right hand exposed so that the sensitive fingertips can detect the sharp edges of tear-opal chunks. Surely your computations have reached the same inevitable conclusion."

Although his accent sounded a bit odd to the pattern

detectors in my circuits, I dismissed it as the result of the droid's age. It was nice to hear a protocol droid code switch into binary, which some humanoid droids considered "primitive." It showed respect.

I nodded. The droid's logic did make sense. My prediction circuits found no harm in giving him a protective suit, one of the few hanging in the mining complex headquarters for occasional inspections by one of the lords of the Gem.

"Thank the Maker!" exclaimed the protocol droid. "And thank *you*."

The silver protocol droid, dressed in a formfitting protective suit, shuffled into the sorting facility awkwardly. These humanoid droids always seemed to move slightly uncertainly, as though the mechanical components could not imitate the movements of organics perfectly.

"Move! Move!" I turned up the volume on my audio digitizer. More and more these days, I was taking on the mannerisms and vocabulary of my masters. I despised myself—the override chip was happy to let me experience these pulses of self-loathing. "Get to the sorting line, now! If you don't pick out a hundred grams of tear opals within an hour, you'll be tossed into the tunnels to dig ore. I doubt your delicate wires would last long in there."

Quietly, the silver droid complied with my order and trotted to the conveyer belt, which carried crushed opal ore past the sorting droids. The two rows of workers bent over the belt and combed through the slush awash in acid for glimpses of the precious gems. From time to time, a droid chirped or yelped as the jagged ore broke through synthetic skin or the acid soaked through to a raw wire, but all the droids pressed on to work as fast as possible, for at the first sign that they were unable to work, they'd be tossed into the tunnels.

The protocol droid found an opening between a squat orange PO5 entertainment unit and a tall cylindrical KT8 cooking unit. His right hand protruded unprotected from the sleeve of the environment suit, and as he sorted through the ore on the belt, he looked across at the silver-and-blue figure of R2-D2 on the other side.

The little astromech was in bad shape. Two of his manipulators had been destroyed by acid, and he was using a single manipulator arm protruding from his barrel body to pick through the ore listlessly. Rocks and rubble had gotten into his treads, so he could no longer move with the grace he had once possessed. He knew his time was limited, and even his posture looked dejected.

"Artoo," the protocol droid said, "I'm here. Sorry it took me so long." There was a cool confidence and sorrow in his voice that seemed out of place in that scorching, pressure-filled, hellish sorting room.

I rolled closer. Was the protocol droid going to be trouble? I wondered if I had made a mistake in allowing him to wear a protective suit.

R2-D2 froze in place as his circuits processed the voice. He seemed unable to believe what he was hearing. As he turned his lone dark photoreceptor toward the protocol droid, he trembled all over. Then he let out a series of shocked chirps and tweeps.

"Calm down," said the protocol droid soothingly. Then he winked with one of his round photoreceptors. "I'm going to get you out of here."

R2-D2 chirped questioningly.

My pattern detectors flared with alarm. Winking was a gesture that should not have been possible for a droid of his model and make.

The dark compulsion rose in me. This was a rebellion being plotted. I had to stop them.

"What are you doing?" I vocalized at high power.

A sword of light materialized in the silver droid's

hands. He jumped high into the air, tumbled backward in an arc over my head, and swung the humming sword down.

Sparks exploded and I knew without having to look that he had sliced off my left arm. The pain was exactly like what I had experienced when they had welded the electric shockers onto my arms.

I struggled to turn, to keep him in sight. The protocol droid landed on his feet, his motion fluid and graceful, completely different from his earlier clumsy shuffle. My sliced-off left arm lay at his feet, a useless hunk of metal sputtering sparks from the end. I had never seen a droid move like that. My pattern detectors concluded that he was an organic, a human.

But that was impossible.

The dark compulsion surged in my processors again, pushing me to complete my mission. I activated my sirens at full volume to call for other enforcers, and I rushed at the silver droid. Even with only one arm, I still had the advantage of mass, speed, and size.

He tried to leap out of the way, but he couldn't gain any purchase as his slick metal feet slipped against the ground strewn with debris and acid wash—the bipedal form was never a very stable design for droids. I collided with him and tackled him to the floor, the sword of light rolling out of his hand. The thrumming blade went out.

I seized him about the neck with my remaining arm. The protective suit he wore was an excellent insulator, rendering my electric shocker ineffective. But the pincers at the end of my arm, capable of demolishing composite walls and bending reinforced metal bars, would crush his neck.

I lifted him into the air, bringing his face even with my photoreceptors. I wanted to gaze into his photoreceptors and see the spark of life go out as I severed the wiring and tubing from his torso to his processors.

He kicked at my thick torso ineffectively, a mere sandypede larva wriggling in the clutches of the iron beak of a steelpecker. I increased the pressure on my pincers.

His hands flew up and grabbed on to my pincers, trying to hold them off. What a useless gesture. I gazed casually at his hands, noting how his left hand was still in the protective environment suit, while the right was exposed. During the struggle earlier, he had tried to cushion his fall with his right hand, and it had dipped into a puddle of acid. The acid had eaten away the plating over his right hand—it must have been synthetic skin that was painted to resemble chrome—to reveal the metal skeleton and wires beneath. I theorized that his hand was so fragile because it was highly sensitive, and he needed it unprotected so that he could operate the lightsaber.

I looked up into his face again to finish him off. But

my pattern recognizers could not process what I was seeing.

My crushing pincers had distorted the plating over his face, cracking the metal shell. Under the transparent helmet of his environment suit, I saw a human face.

Everything fell into place. That was why he had tricked U'rum into not applying the restraining harness; that was why he needed the protective suit. He was not a droid at all.

But then I looked back at the metallic skeletal hand clutching at my pincer; I looked back into the eyes of the man dying in front of me. There was no fear or terror in his face, only determination. How was that possible? Was he droid or man?

My hesitation caused my grip to relax slightly. Taking advantage of the moment, the man-droid cried out in binary, "We have to work together! This is your last chance to be free!"

R2-D2 whistled loudly and charged forward. A

manipulator arm, until then hidden, emerged from his cylindrical torso. As he crashed into me, sparks flew from the end of the arm, zapping into my legs.

It was so weak that I couldn't even feel it. But the gesture seemed to awaken the rest of the droids in the sorting facility. A second earlier, they had been watching the fight in front of them as a stunned audience; now they realized they were players.

Some of the droids rushed to the entrances of the tunnels and brought down the blast doors to keep out other enforcer droids. Others gathered around me, attacking me as a mob. Still other droids had the idea of breaking down the conveyor belt and using the struts as levers to pry me off balance. A clever idea, but it would be too slow.

There was a reason Lady Eekee had made me an enforcer. The puny limbs of the rebel droids had no effect on me. I increased the pressure around the man-droid's neck and choked off any more speeches from him. I could see his face turn dark red from the lack of air and his eyes bulge from the pressure. Still, I saw no despair.

A part of me that I thought had long been expunged from my circuits sparked back to life. It was tiny, weak, as hopeless as their rebellion. But the utter fearlessness in the man-droid's face gave that part of me courage. Once again, I pushed back against the darkness in my processors, and the pincers stopped where they were. I could not hold them steady forever, but it felt like a triumph just to assert my will even for a moment.

The man-droid took advantage of the momentary pause to choke out a command. "Artoo, the saber. It's stuck!"

R2-D2, after spinning in place for a few seconds, made a beeline for a spot on the floor. Frantically, he dug through a pile of rubble and picked up something.

He chirped excitedly at the man-droid in my clutches.

And that was how I finally learned the name of the man-droid. Translated into Basic, what R2-D2 said was: *Luke, catch!*

The darkness in me was an overwhelming flood. My rekindled will crumbled under its pressure. The pincers once again squeezed hard against the man-droid's neck.

A cylindrical object sailed through the air, flipping from end to end. The man-droid wriggling at the end of my pincers reached out with his right hand and caught it.

Fwummmm.

The lightsaber reignited, and one second later my right arm was also gone. At that moment, the droids leaning on the strut levers finally succeeded in their plan and I tumbled to the ground.

Droids gathered around me. I looked up helplessly into the faces of the protocol droids, the entertainment droids, the cleaners and cooks and librarians and nannies. I had tortured them for weeks in that hellish facility, forcing them to bend to the will of the lords of the Gem. It was time for them to exact their vengeance.

Several small droids stumbled over, a massive rock suspended between their arms. They wanted to drop it on my head and crush my processors into oblivion.

I shut off my photoreceptors. I didn't need to watch my own end. I almost welcomed it.

"No!"

I activated my photoreceptors again. The man-droid—Luke—was standing above me, lightsaber at the ready. He was holding off the droids who were intent on killing me, the evil enforcer.

"There's still good in her," he said. "I know it."

R2-D2 beeped indignantly.

"It's *not* because of the Force," Luke said. "I'm pretty handy with machines, you know?"

He beckoned to R2-D2, who came over reluctantly.

Luke directed him to the hidden access panel at the back of my processor housing. "Artoo, cut here. Be careful."

I could feel R2-D2 and Luke working together to remove the override chip and rewire my empathy circuits. It was difficult, delicate work, and they were taking a long time.

Loud banging came from the tunnels. Tongues of flames appeared in the blast doors. The enforcer droids were breaking through. The other droids in the room chattered over each other.

"We have to leave, *now*!"

"They're going to deactivate all of us and toss us into the acid pools! Oh, Maker—"

"Should have killed her when we had the chance—"

"It's too late. We're doomed. Doomed!"

Luke and Artoo ignored them. They kept on soldering, wiring, connecting, probing—

And just like that, the darkness was gone from me.

I let out a long trembling whistle, an electronic sob. I turned my head to look at them.

"Are you an engineer?" I asked. From the way he had been talking to Artoo, it seemed that even without the translation circuitry in his disguise, he could speak binary—or at least understand some of it.

"Not exactly," said Luke, smiling. "But I did always like to tinker with machines. Artoo here did most of the work."

"Are you . . . a droid or a man?" I asked.

But Luke didn't hear me. One of the blast doors exploded open, and a hulking enforcer droid, even more massive than I, emerged from the tunnel. He was dripping with acid, and his photoreceptors glowed fiery red. He raised his twin blasters and aimed them at the droids in the room. Those would kill, not merely disable.

The cacophony died down. The rebelling droids cowered, waiting for the inevitable.

But Luke stood where he was, as calm as a tree stump.

The enforcer fired. Twin bolts headed straight for Luke.

The lightsaber jumped up from the floor, where Luke had left it, leapt into Luke's machine hand, and came to life. In a single, graceful swing that was impossibly fast, Luke deflected the two bolts and sent them heading straight back at the enforcer droid. The bolts struck the droid's legs, and he collapsed where he stood.

The other droids in the room cheered. But the enforcer droid was still moving on the ground, pushing himself up with his arms, compelled by the dark urges implanted in his processors to hurt and harm again.

"Don't kill him," I said. My digitizer fluctuated as current surged through my empathy circuits, making the words sound distorted. "Please. He's just like me. There's goodness still in him."

Luke leaned down, and for the first time I saw sorrow in his eyes. "I know. But there's no time for me and Artoo to help all the enforcers the way we helped you."

"If only there were a way to get to the Parity Gate," I whispered.

"What do you mean?"

So I explained to him Lady Eekee's deliberate use of inelegant and crude programming techniques in the override chip. I told him that there was an obvious weakness, a single logic gate that could be flipped to disable the whole chip.

It would be a fast programming modification. But it was so delicate and required such precision that no droid could perform the operation, let alone a human. Lady Eekee had dangled the weakness in front of me as a taunt, just another way to crush my resistance, because there was no way to exploit that weakness.

But Luke smiled and said, "Thank you."

The enforcer droid was on his elbows. He aimed the blasters again.

Luke stood up. Instead of crouching in a defensive stance, he deactivated the lightsaber. Electronic gasps came from all over the room.

Luke closed his eyes and reached out with his hands, as though manipulating invisible switches in the air.

The other droids and I looked at each other, utterly baffled. But Artoo whistled as though it were the most ordinary thing in the world. "He's using the Force."

A droid who could command the mystical energy called the Force? I didn't know what to think.

I watched the enforcer droid in the broken doorway with terrified fascination. He was steadying his position . . . he was taking aim . . . he was pulling the trigger. . . .

He let go and dropped back to the ground, a long electronic whistle emerging from his digitizer.

Above me, Luke opened his eyes and broke into a wide grin. "I got them. All of them. Just the way you taught me."

The banging noises in the tunnels had ceased, and the cutting torches were no longer cleaving the blast doors.

Gingerly, the other droids opened the blast doors, and the enforcer droids emerged, beeping and chirping with joy and disbelief. Luke had disabled their override chips without seeing them or touching them. He had just . . . reached out.

"I closed the Parity Gates," he said, as if flipping a few dozen minuscule logic gates scattered across trillions of gates in enforcer droids all over the Deep with his mind alone weren't magic, weren't simply incredible. He had done what no organic and no droid could have done. It was a miracle.

More slave droids streamed out of the tunnels, many of them barely functioning.

"Let's get out of here," Luke said. And the wave of chirps and beeps and whistles that greeted that announcement was the most beautiful binary music I had ever heard.

We took every available freight skiff back up to the Gem, and I was sure our ride was smooth because Luke piloted it. There seemed nothing out of the realm of possibility when he was involved.

Following Luke's directions, the army of rebel droids soon secured the whole station. The surprised lords and ladies of the Deep were cuffed and put into the cages on U'rum's ship. I particularly enjoyed watching the hate-filled face of Lord Kluleyeke as Artoo stuffed a glue gag deep into his mandibles, preventing him from making another speech about noble sacrifices and his refined tastes.

The plan was for Luke to take us back to our home worlds on U'rum's ship. He said he would make a stop along the way to drop off the lords and ladies of the Gem with the authorities so they could be put on trial. I promised to show up as a witness.

Luke, who had removed his protocol droid disguise, reattached a pair of construction arms to me. They felt strange, and I flexed the appendages uncertainly.

"You'll get used to them," he said. "I know how it feels." He flexed his right hand, covered by a glove.

Artoo and Luke headed for the cockpit, looking for all the world like an ordinary human pilot and his astromech droid.

I've made many tree-stump carvings of the pair since then, and I tell anyone who asks that they are of the great Jedi Luke Skywalker, who once freed thousands of slaves on a forgotten world.

But I know a deeper truth. Luke Skywalker is not merely a great man; he is also, at least partly, a great droid.

INTERLUDE FOUR

"I WANT TO HEAR MORE STORIES about droid heroes in the future," said G'kolu. "Thank you, Geetoo."

The others in the galley agreed. The ancient droid beeped an acknowledgment.

Time to move on.

Flux took a deep breath. "Is there no other choice?" She looked with trepidation into the yawning maw of the dark chute that led to the bilge. The odor of rotting garbage and pungent machine grease wafted up from the hidden depths.

Just then, all the lights on the mess deck turned on in unison. The bright glare made everyone squint. The humming of the ship's engines shifted to a deeper rumble.

"I think we just came out of hyperspace," said Teal, more experienced than the other deckhands.

Speakers came to life throughout the ship as Tuuma the Hutt's growling voice filled the air.

"Attention, crew members: We've been intercepted by a Cantonica customs patrol for a surprise visit. All deckhands should remain where they are as officers make a final sweep of the ship before the inspectors come aboard to make sure that everything is . . . orderly."

"He means that the officers need to prepare the bribes and get the smuggled goods out of sight," hissed Teal.

Footsteps echoed in the corridors, and the fathiers moaned and growled nervously.

"You gotta go!" Teal snapped at Flux.

"All right," said Flux. "But will you come with me? I'll be too scared down there alone."

Teal hesitated. "But—"

"It must mean something that we shared stories

tonight," said Flux. "I can't explain it, but I believe the Tide wants us to be together."

Teal bit her lip and nodded. "Fine. I doubt Tuuma will check the bunks while the ship is being turned upside down by inspectors."

"EEP-ding tick OOP ding-ding TWEEP," beeped G2-X.

Tyra turned to Teal and Flux. "He says he needs to go with you. There are sludge-cleaning droids and maintenance systems down there that could hurt you. He can help."

"Thank you, Geetoo," said Flux. She placed a hand over the squat form of the droid custodian affectionately.

"What's going on here?" asked G'kolu. "When did the bilge become the most popular part of the ship?"

The pounding of the footsteps in the corridors grew louder, intermixed with the first mate's impatient voice. "Check the mess deck. . . . One of the deckhands spilled something down there last night. . . . Make sure it's cleaned up and the contraband spices in the pantry are hidden. . . ."

"I think I need to go with you," said Tyra to Flux. "I don't like to be seen by . . . officials. Besides, I can help you down there. We scavengers are good to have around whenever garbage heaps are involved, and I can help you talk to the droids."

"Hey! I'm not going to stay here all by myself," said G'kolu. "How am I supposed to explain why I've been here half the night when I was supposed to just clean up and go back to sleep?"

"What happened to 'the Grease'?" said Tyra, her voice cracking with mirth. "I thought you were the expert on smooth talking."

The footsteps were just outside the entrance to the mess deck.

"All right! No more bickering," said Teal. "We're all going into the bilge."

One by one, they grabbed the top of the chute and jumped in.

Total, complete darkness.

Splash. Burble. Pitter-patter. Plop.

"Oh, the smell!"

"This is so much worse than I thought."

"Even piles of rotting fish and shells is better than this—"

"What was that thing that just brushed my legs? I think it had scales!"

"Just give it a hard kick. Bilge-water lobsters are harmless—"

"Keep going! Keep going! There should be a platform out of this sludge in the bow."

"EEP! EEP! Ack-ackackack."

"I'm going to throw up if we stay here much longer."

"Quiet! Do you want to make so much noise in here that the customs inspectors come down? Just stop thinking about the smell. Breathe through your mouth and pinch your nose."

"I smell through my horns."

"Oh . . . I didn't know that."

"There's a lot you don't know about the Grease."

"I'll be sure to set aside time after this to study the legends of Your Smoothness."

"I've got to be distracted. Help me."

"How do you want us to distract you? Don't ask me to sing."

"I won't—I've heard you in the shower. . . . How about you tell me a story?"

"You want *me* to tell a story?"

"Sure. You must know some good stories, considering how much you like to talk. Tell me a story about . . . Luke Skywalker. That seems to be the theme tonight."

"It's the Tide."

"Oh, enough with the Tide!"

"Start talking, Teal! I need a Luke Skywalker story to keep my mind off this stench!"

"All right . . . I don't know if this story is true. But I did hear it from one of the most interesting characters I've ever met. . . ."

SIZE MATTERS NOT. LOOK AT ME.
JUDGE ME BY MY SIZE, DO YOU?
—YODA

THE TALE OF
LUGUBRIOUS MOTE

IT'S TOUGH BEING SMALL.

A curious fact of life in the galaxy is that most sentient species are about the same size: ranging in height between about half a meter to three meters. This fundamental assumption about scale in most designers' minds can be observed in the ceiling height of wretched, scum-ridden cantinas on backwater planets like Tatooine, as well as the size of the repulsorpods in the ancient Grand Convocation Chamber of the Galactic Senate.

Anyone under this typical range is often looked down on. Literally.

That is why Kowakian monkey-lizards, smaller than human infants, get no respect in most corners of the galaxy. Even the most famous Kowakian monkey-lizard of them all, Salacious B. Crumb, widely acclaimed by his own kind as a master comedian, skilled in both physical antics and verbal whimsy, could not be accepted among the upper echelon of society. He had to settle as court jester to the terrible and butyraceous Jabba the Hutt.

See, you've never even heard of Salacious, have you? But your eyebrows lifted at the mention of Jabba, the peerless crime lord.

Surprised at my vocabulary, are you? Did not expect sesquipedalian words to emerge from my half-centimeter body? Oh, how predictable you are.

I'm Lugubrious Mote, the real source of Salacious Crumb's comedic genius, and this is my tale.

Splash. Burble. Pitter-patter. Plop.

"Wait, wait! What do these words mean? I've never even heard some of them."

"I told you the story is from a most unusual teller."

"Sounds like she just likes big words."

"Ha, you're not entirely wrong. A sesquipedalian word is a really long word, one spelled with enough letters to go around the page a few times. For such a small creature, she had extraordinary lung capacity."

"At least my brain is sufficiently distracted that I can almost forget the smell around here. . . ."

"Jabba didn't smell much better, from what I understand."

"What about 'buty-,' um, 'buty-ra'—"

"You don't need to understand every word to understand a story. In fact, the most important parts of stories aren't always told in words. Just follow along."

First, observe and admire my form. I know I'm a bit hard to see, so feel free to use the magnifying glass hanging next to my ten-centimeter stage. Take note that my body is just a hair under four millimeters long, and from an ovoid torso covered in chitinous carapace extend two pairs of furry legs, a pair of smooth segmented arms ending in opposable pincers, and a pulchritudinous, whiskered head. Like other females of my species, I can jump as high as a meter from standing still, and I can lift forty times my bodyweight.

Biologists from the University of Coruscant describe my species, the mole-fleas of Kowak, as parasites, but that's hardly fair. We think of ourselves as living in an ancient arrangement of mutual benefit with the monkey-lizards. In the lush, dense forests of Kowak, each monkey-lizard has living on its body a colony of mole-fleas who advise it on relations with the other monkey-lizards, warn it of danger, and keep its skin and hair free of harmful, true parasites. When infant monkey-lizards are born, some mole-fleas from each parent migrate to the young creature to set up a new colony, and thereby give the child the wisdom and experience of the mole-flea communities of both parents.

Our civilization evolved in conjunction with theirs, and I daresay our civilization is the more sophisticated for the simple reason that our minds are far quicker than theirs, just as our movements are far nimbler. We mole-fleas may live a life only a tenth as long as the average monkey-lizard, but we squeeze just as much delight and sorrow into it. To do so, we live a single day as though it were a week, and in the time it takes a monkey-lizard brain to think and say one word, we've composed a sentence out of ten words.

To compensate for our small stature, nature gave us outsize brains and accelerated nerves.

I grew up on Salacious Crumb. When Salacious first decided to leave Kowak to seek his fortune, my colony held a meeting and decided that they didn't want to go into the uncertainties of space. Instead, members of the colony would scatter to join their relatives on other hosts. I was the only one who decided to accompany Salacious on his adventure.

"I want a full partnership," I told him.

He cackled for five minutes. I took that as an inept expression of gratitude.

See, here's the thing: Salacious was a natural performer, and he was blessed with a panoply of physical features suitable for a crowd-pleasing clown: floppy ears, messy hair, wide-and-oh-so-hypnotic eyes, gangly limbs, clumsy movements, and an infectious cackle. But he didn't possess much of a brain between those outsize ears.

He couldn't write any jokes, because he was dumber than a newborn rancor.

I was the one who came up with all his material, including the monkey poodoo jokes. I also had to sit in the nest of hair on top of his head and whisper the jokes into his big ears because he couldn't memorize them.

So why didn't I go into the comedy business myself if I was so clever? you ask. Comedy requires a certain willingness to look like a fool, to suffer humiliation, to scrape and bow, to use small words. You've heard my eloquence—I don't have the temperament for it.

That's why I thought the two of us would make a great team.

The trouble was, few outside of Kowak understood the screeching language of the monkey-lizards, and working through an interpreter was death for any comedian. (You've dealt with protocol droids, haven't you? They're insufferable.)

To rescue Salacious's nonexistent career, I advised him to turn himself into a physical comedian. Pratfalls and slapstick are the universal language of comedy. I came up with a whole routine of tumbles, slips, falls, leaps, twirls, handstands, spit takes, fake choking, and pantomimed shocks.

But Salacious was a terrible student. He was so uncoordinated and clumsy that he couldn't do many of the flips and slides I had choreographed for him. After many seconds of hard thinking, I came up with the idea of sitting on top of his head, like the pilot of one of those AT-AT walkers we once saw at a spaceport under martial law, and sending him signals for how to move by biting him in different spots on his head. That was the only way he could move with enough coordination to chew a snapping fish bladder while also dancing like an inebriated Gamorrean—trust me, it was a funny move.

He couldn't help cackling at his own jokes though, which ruined a lot of the effect.

But humor is subjective, and despite all odds, the gangster boss Jabba the Hutt took a liking to him—particularly his cackling. Salacious took credit for the whole thing and never even mentioned me to His August Corpulency. Some partner he turned out to be.

Then again, considering Salacious had to amuse Jabba at least once a day to get his food and drink—and I got to share in the crumbs—lest the oversize slug kill him, maybe it was a good thing that I was beneath Jabba's notice.

For a long time I lived in Salacious's hair and helped him survive at the crime lord's pleasure. At night I hopped about the palace and listened to the talk of bounty hunters and smugglers who came to bargain with the oily oversize sausage. I learned a lot about the galaxy, even if I didn't get to see every corner of it. It wasn't the life of adventure I was promised, but I thought I was content.

Until the day Skywalker showed up.

Picture me in my nest, woven from thick vines, each of which was the width of my legs. Instead of plant fibers, the vines were made from keratin, colored the same shade of tannish puce that dominated everything on the desert planet of Tatooine. The vines were hard to work with: stubborn, inflexible, and utterly lacking in the kind of yielding softness desirable in good bedding. The thick strands emerged from the dry, leathery ground, and I had to introduce some pliancy into that most uncooperative material with judicious nicks from my teeth.

My teeth were hurting that morning because I'd had to chew through several extra-thick keratin vines to soften them up—maintaining the structural integrity of my nest was a constant struggle as the strands grew without cease, and new cuts had to be made every few days lest my nest unwind itself.

Might as well give you a climate and seismic activity report. The sky was its usual, perpetually hazy murk unbroken by the light of the twin suns or the twinkle of stars—since Mount Jabba didn't like being outside much, Salacious Ridge, my host and habitat, couldn't go outside, either. Earlier that day, chunks of the remains of some unfortunate creature slathered in slime and digestive juices had rained down in the vine forest, and a flash storm consisting of sour wine and fermented fruit juices had carved rivulets in the dry ground. Despite my disgust, I emerged from my nest to scavenge what edible bits of flesh I could find—oh, how shameful I would appear in the eyes of my home tribe! And then I had to scramble to clear out what I couldn't eat or drink by tossing the excess chunks off the sheer cliff face beyond the vine forest, lest the nest turn into a smelly, swampy mess. To get a bit of exercise, I hop-climbed Left-Ear Peak and Right-Ear Peak with some rotting carrion as free weights.

A vile-smelling mist rolled in and clouded over everything. All I could do was retreat into my nest and hold my breath, coughing in fits when it got to be too much. Overhead, thunderous snores and roaring laughter alternated in unpredictable waves, forcing me to cover my delicate ears as my whiskers twitched in annoyance. Under me, my host reacted by quaking like the deck of some storm-tossed ship, with a high-pitched cackling that sounded like the ground itself was being torn asunder.

All in all, just a typical day in the tangled hair-jungle atop the head of Salacious Crumb and beneath the looming mountain of flesh and fat that was Jabba the Hutt.

"Can't you shield me from the hookah smoke?" I begged Salacious. "Put on a hat or something." Of all Jabba's disgusting habits, that was the worst. The smoke got into Salacious's hair and there was nothing I could do to get the smell out.

Salacious made no reply except stamping his foot, grinding it into the ground, and then cackling maniacally. The message was clear: if I made myself known, he would do nothing to protect me, and I would be squashed like a common, insensate flea.

I was thinking of some clever insult for Salacious—sometimes it took him days to work out what I meant—when a flash of lightning split the murk in the distance and a gargantuan, glowing man-star flickered into existence like an exploding supernova, lighting up half the sky. He was so huge that he loomed over the bulk of Jabba like the ten-thousand-year-old pasol tree shading the slick rock that was Salacious Crumb's hide-out back on Kowak. He was like an ancient god from the creation myths, there in the flesh. I hopped onto the tip of Salacious's ear to get a better look.

"Greetings, Exalted One. . . ."

I had never heard a voice like that: sonorous and resonant, at once pleading and threatening, suffused with a confidence that seemed indistinguishable from swagger. The hubbub of Jabba's court quieted as I had never remembered the place quieting, and the glowing man-star went on.

"I am Luke Skywalker, Jedi Knight and friend of Captain Solo. I seek an audience with Your Greatness, to bargain for his life. . . ."

The booming figure flickered. I realized that this Luke Skywalker was not real but an illusion projected from the top of a dome-headed blue-and-silver droid standing next to a golden human-formed droid companion. They were gifts to Jabba from this Skywalker, apparently. He was submitting to Jabba before even arriving; I couldn't help being disappointed.

My time in Jabba's palace had shown me plenty of sycophants and frauds and con artists. This Skywalker, however, presented a bit of a conundrum. On the one hand, he wasn't even brave enough to show up in person and was just as cloying and meek in his approach to the Hutt gangster as any lowlife criminal. On the other hand, he wasn't there to bargain for profit or some unsavory favor from Jabba but to plead for his friend, which endeared him to me a little.

Was he just foolhardy or running some big con? I wondered.

He was an uncertainty wrapped within an enigma hidden within a mystery.

After Luke made a splash with his hologram, nothing new happened for a while, and life in Jabba's palace fell back into its usual routine of disgusting food, smelly smoke, and an endless stream of obsequious toadies. I tried to get Salacious Crumb to vary his routine a bit—I was sick of the old slapstick—but he adamantly refused.

"Trying something new could get you a promotion," I whispered in his left ear.

He cackled at some idiotic, witless comment from Jabba and scratched at his ear to make me go away.

My host had no ambition. *Sigh.*

I took to roaming the palace, even during the day. One could take only so much of living under the dripping chin of that mountain of malignant flesh. I felt the ground shake as Jabba's band shifted from one musical style to another in a vain effort to excite that sluggish brain. I held my tongue as I clung to the wall and observed the grotesque henchmen vying with one another to laugh the loudest as Jabba tortured his hapless slave, Oola the dancer. Salacious had the dubious honor of being the leader in that competition. I hopped through Jabba's treasury and examined his collection of exquisite loot—unfortunately marred by the slime from his grubby hands.

And then everything turned topsy-turvy with the arrival of Leia.

Never mind the bold gambit with the Wookiee prisoner, the preposterous disguise, and the clicking thermal detonator. Never mind the sheer audacity of navigating Jabba's palace in the dark and stealing his most prized possession from right under Jabba's nose. Never mind the fact that by the standards of most sapient creatures, Leia's plan was absolutely mad.

The thing I most admired about her? How calm she was after her plan failed.

The absurd outfit that Jabba made her wear was designed to wear her down, break her resistance. It was too cold for the ambient temperature of the palace, and it exposed her to constant harassment from the Hutt. Jabba was practically an artist when it came to using disgust and humiliation as weapons. Countless enemies who would never have given in to mere pain broke down under the Hutt lord's vile mind games.

But watching her, you'd never know Leia was bothered by any of it. She was utterly calm. Reclining at the center of the hectic, repugnant maelstrom that was Jabba's court, she was an untouchable center of tranquility. Though she was Jabba's prisoner, she acted like a princess, a queen.

I had never seen such grace in a human. *Jabba could not defeat her.*

Later, in the darkness, as Jabba, Salacious, and the rest of the court lay asleep, I hopped out of my nest atop the monkey-lizard. With a single bound, I landed in Leia's hair, which, I noted with some wistfulness, seemed far more comfortable and reminded me of the soft moss back on Kowak that I used to mix with Salacious's rough hair to give myself a homey touch. That intricate bun on top of her head would make a nice bell tower, and the long braid would be a fantastic staircase.

But enough real estate fantasies. I had a mission.

"*Pssst,*" I whispered into Leia's ear. "You awake?"

Her eyes snapped open in the dark. "Who's there?"

"Your mistake," I said, "was to see Jabba as an equal." I didn't answer her question directly because in my experience, as soon as people saw me, they stopped listening.

"Explain yourself." Her tone wasn't defensive or angry. "And slow down. I can barely understand you."

Right. I kept on forgetting how slow these big creatures were. I had to slow down my speech by a factor of ten to make my Galactic Basic comprehensible to the average human.

I enunciated each syllable deliberately, dragging my words out. I thought I sounded like a glitchy holo recording that skipped and stuttered, but I couldn't afford to be impatient. "You wan-der-ed through his pa-la-ce like a thief, but you for-got that he *is* a great thief. Of course he caught you."

"That's a reasonable point," she said. "What would you have done?"

"A flea can drink the blood of a fathier because the flea is almost invisible to the great beast," I said.

"Show yourself," she said. "I like to see who I'm talking to."

I hopped onto the tip of her nose, ready to leap away if she swatted at me, as I fully expected her to.

She didn't. Instead, she gazed at me, cross-eyed in the darkness, and smiled.

So that was how one of the most unlikely of alliances, between a mole-flea of Kowak and a princess of the House of Organa, was struck.

She told me about stars that dealt death, about the darkness deeper than space that was the Empire, about the nascent pinpricks of light of the Rebel Alliance, about the grand vision of a free galaxy.

"There will be a seat for everyone in the Senate

chamber, no matter their wealth, power, or language," she declared. "Or size," she added after a second.

And I imagined colonies of mole-fleas spreading across the galaxy, advising hosts who were generals, senators, moguls, opera singers, perhaps even princesses. I told her of my wish.

"I'm not sure I would be the most suitable host," she said diplomatically. "If you were living on me, my scalp would get awfully itchy. But . . . I'm certain we can find you another willing host."

Mollified, I offered her my aid.

"Luke is coming," she said. "Give him your aid. He's our best hope."

"The illusion-man?" I asked skeptically.

"He'll grow on you," she said, her eyes twinkling. "You'll see."

"I must be allowed to speak," the hooded figure said from the shadows. His voice was odd, toneless. The monsters of Jabba's court stirred uneasily in the murk.

Jabba's eyes snapped open in the haze above me like Tatooine's twin suns. A torrent of slimy drool poured out of the cavernous mouth overhead and splashed into the dirty hair atop Salacious, who let out a half-hearted cackle.

It was no time for comedy. I jumped out of the way at the last second and landed on Leia's shoulder. As Jabba continued to thunder bombastically above me, I scrambled to a perch right below Leia's right ear.

"He must be allowed to speak," said Bib Fortuna, the Hutt's craven majordomo.

There was something wrong with his voice. It sounded even more soulless than usual.

"He's using an old Jedi mind trick," roared the Hutt. He tossed Bib Fortuna out of the way.

I was confused. The Jedi were figures of legend,

and I never really believed they had magical powers. But it was possible that they knew something about hypnosis—something I had seen street magicians perform for the crowd. Maybe Luke had learned such a trick. I just hoped he didn't have an overinflated opinion of its efficacy.

Jabba was speaking so slowly that I had enough time to dodge a few more drops of drool, each bigger than I was. How Leia could stand the stench was beyond me.

"You will bring Captain Solo and the Wookiee to me," said the hooded figure in that same toneless voice. He took a step forward into the light and removed the cowl hiding his face.

Like other humans, he was gigantic—though only in an average sort of way. Also, like all large creatures, his face was pockmarked by imperfections—perfect footholds and handholds if I were to choose to scale the cliff of his cheeks to get to his hair for nesting. Unlike the hologram version, in real life he had a boyish look and a sort of easy confidence that told me right away he was doomed.

"He has no idea what he's doing, does he?" I whispered into Leia's ear.

Leia tensed. I could see that she wasn't sure what Luke was planning, either.

"You sound like a buzzing mosquito," she hissed. "I can't understand a thing you're saying."

Right. I had forgotten again. "He knows one trick, and he thinks that's e-nough." I forced myself to slow down and *really* articulate. "O-ver-con-fi-dent. He's ma-king the same mis-take *you* made."

Above me came the thunderclaps of Jabba's roaring laughter, heartier than any Salacious had ever caused. The poor monkey-lizard tried to cackle to support his master's mirth, but the pitiful noises were drowned out by Jabba's dominant guffaws.

"Jabba makes his living by devouring forgers, con men, and liars. He knows more mind tricks than anyone."

By the way Leia's jaws clenched, I could tell that she understood the trouble Luke was in.

I saw Luke catch Leia's gaze, and the glow of confidence went out of his eyes. He looked like a little boy, lost. I felt a wave of pity for him.

Why were members of the large sentient species so foolish? So arrogant? Why were they blind to what was so obvious to me?

Jabba mocked the young Skywalker for his foolhardy nonplan, and as his fetid breath washed over her in waves, Leia flinched. I knew that faith was dying in her heart, as well.

I feared the worst as Luke took another step forward, moving even closer to Leia and Jabba. "Nevertheless, I'm taking Captain Solo and his friends. You can either profit by this or be destroyed." His expression was determined, as if he fully believed every word he was saying.

Even if he was foolish and overconfident, I admired

the fact that he wouldn't give up. In that, he and Leia were very much alike.

"I told you he'll grow on you," said Leia. Her voice was so low that only I could hear her.

"The only thing growing is my confidence that he's in over his head," I said, my eyes focused on the spot Luke was standing on. "Don't you understand what's happening? Jabba is reeling him in; he's—"

"Master Luke," C-3PO, the protocol droid, broke in. "You're standing on—"

Leia's own warning as she realized the truth was choked off as Jabba jerked the chain attached to her collar.

"I shall enjoy watching you die," said Jabba, guffawing.

Confused and desperate, Luke lunged at one of the guards standing next to Bib Fortuna and somehow— to this day, I'm still not sure how he did it—the guard's blaster flew out of its holster and leapt into Luke's hand.

Now, I'm sure plenty of people hearing my story will tell you this was proof that Luke had facility with "the Force," that mysterious, magical power that everyone loves to drone on and on about ("Oh, it pervades the galaxy!" "Oooo, it allowed the Jedi to protect the Republic!" "Ahhhh, it can do anything!"). But the truth is, there's no such thing as "the Force." I'm a consummate rationalist, and I believe only what can be seen and touched.

My best working theory is that the guard was another one of Luke's friends who infiltrated Jabba's palace; you wouldn't believe how many of his co-conspirators managed to make their way in there just like Leia. But anyway, I digress.

Here's what happened next, in the span of about a second:

Luke grabbed the blaster ineptly, as if it were a hot thermal detonator, and—

Before he could even get off a single shot, one of Jabba's Gamorrean guards grabbed him from behind—

Jabba slammed home the switch that released the trapdoor at the foot of his throne—

There followed a clumsy struggle between the colossal Gamorrean and the gigantic Luke that seemed to last forever—a frustrating scene for a nimble-footed, agile athlete like me to watch—

A bolt shot out of Luke's blaster and struck the ceiling, setting off a shower of sparks, which I had no trouble dodging since I was so quick, but it did burn Leia's skin. She gritted her teeth—

Luke fell through the yawning hole in the ground—

Salacious cackled insipidly—

The Gamorrean, his prey having suddenly slipped out of his grasp, lost his balance and held on precariously to the edge of Jabba's throne—

But that second was plenty of time for a quick mind like mine to work through the implications. Princess Leia was going to lose her champion unless I did something. This was my one and only chance to change the odds in her favor and prove my worth as an ally. Also, since I had always thought of myself as the brains of the partnership between Salacious and me, maybe it was time I proved that I could perform as big as I talked.

Well, maybe *big* wasn't quite the right word.

As the Gamorrean teetered precariously above the pit, I made up my mind to go on my quest to save Luke Skywalker. He was a clumsy, foolish, and rash boy, but he was brave and his heart was in the right place.

I leapt from Leia's shoulder onto the back of the Gamorrean, and as soon as I landed, the porcine beast fell through the trapdoor after Luke.

Salacious cackled maniacally, not yet realizing he had lost the only brain that mattered.

Down, down, down we fell into the darkness.

And abruptly, we emerged into the dank, dim dungeon below Jabba's throne, where only a few rays managed to filter through the grille in the high ceiling through which Jabba enjoyed watching his victims die.

With an earsplitting screech, the heavy door at the end of the dungeon rose to reveal the horror hidden behind: Jabba's rancor.

Imagine a creature half of whose body mass is taken up by a massive, cave-like maw filled with stalactites and stalagmites of teeth. Imagine also a pair of powerful arms ending in sharp claws taking up half of the rest. Finally, imagine that this nightmarish creature dwarfed a human as much as Salacious Crumb dwarfed me.

Luke scrambled to his feet, the bravado on his face replaced by helpless terror. The Gamorrean guard I was riding completely forgot about his duty. All he wanted was to climb back up the slick chute through which he had fallen.

You probably think I was so terrified that all I could do was hold on to the Gamorrean and pray to die as quickly as possible.

On the contrary, I had never been so delighted.

Remember, you are thinking at your scale, not mine.

A flea can drink the blood of a fathier because the flea is almost invisible to the great beast.

At my size, the rancor was nothing but a lumbering mountain that was more habitat than threat. If it had tried to bite me, I would have run laps around the gaps between its teeth. If it had tried to step on me, I would have taken a nap in the deep grooves and wrinkles that marred its leathery skin. Long before it could have gotten a chance to see me, much less catch me, I would have leapt onto its back and built a new home in the folds above its oblivious, swimming-pool eyes.

I was ready to show the rancor who was boss.

But no matter how much I shouted in his ear to stop, turn around, and stand his ground, the Gamorrean wouldn't listen. It was impossible to reason with a Gamorrean—one of many flaws with that species.

So of course the rancor reached down, grabbed him, and swallowed him in a few bites like a juicy frog-fruit.

Above us, Jabba laughed, Salacious cackled, Leia gasped, and Jabba's monstrous court erupted into raucous jeers.

Five easy hops later, I was on Luke's shoulder, and one more leap put me next to his ear. He was still backing up, his terrified gaze focused on the looming monster.

The rancor, having finished its Gamorrean snack, turned clumsily to regard Luke.

"Don't worry," I said into Luke's ear. "You've got this."

I had a whole routine prepared to calm the startled

youth after hearing a disembodied voice. I was going to jump onto his nose so he could get a good look at me, and I was going to explain to him all about the deal I had made with Princess Leia to help the Rebellion. All he had to do was trust me.

But he didn't react the way I thought he would at all. After a momentary shiver from being startled, his body immediately relaxed. He squatted down into a fighting stance, and a smile appeared on his face.

Confused, I asked, "Aren't you going to ask who I am?"

"No," he said. "I know you're the spirit of a Jedi, and you're going to tell me to use the Force."

Oh, dear me.

Before I could explain, the rancor took a shambling step forward. But instead of running, Luke just *stayed* there.

"I'm *so* ready," he said. "Tell me what to do. Maybe I should use my Jedi mind trick? 'This is not the food you're looking for.' Or how about if I use my air-grab powers and *call* two of those teeth from its mouth into my hands and then stab them into its eyes? Oh! I know, I should find a rock and toss it right into its throat *just so* and have it lodge in its gullet so it chokes—"

My whiskers trembled in disbelief, and I slapped my pincers against my forehead.

But there was no time to cure the young man of his delusions. "Step back, back!" I shouted into his ear.

He stumbled back a couple of steps. That wasn't what he was expecting from his ghost Jedi guide, and I could tell by the way he trembled that he was getting nervous.

At least he can follow directions, I thought. Then I realized that this wouldn't be so bad. I could still make it work. Instead of fighting against his instincts, I had to work with them. If I could manage the vapid

Salacious Crumb, surely I could do the same with the overeager Luke.

A quick scan around the distant cave floor from my vantage point gave me a plan.

"Now, reach out with all of your senses, Luke." It was distasteful to play into superstition, but I had to soothe his nerves and gain his trust. "Let the Force move through you and over you. . . . Feel how the Force guides you through your . . . er . . . scalp. . . ."

I jumped onto the top of his head. Bracing myself by grabbing strands of his hair in each of my pincer hands, I sank my microscopic mouthparts—that would be a pair of epidermis-piercing barbs, six sucking tubes, three stirring tentacles, five regurgitation ducts, and seven feeding agitators—gently into Luke's skin. No point in going too fast when you bite a host for the first time.

"Wait! I can feel it," he said, his voice full of awe. "I

can feel the Force tickling me in the back of my head!"

Good. Good. I sank my mouthparts deeper. I wasn't just referring to the fact that my plan was going to work. He actually tasted pretty good.

He turned around; behind us, the rancor had taken another step forward.

"This wasn't quite how it worked the last time," he said. "Obi-Wan never made my scalp itch—Ouch!"

I was too far from his ear to make myself heard, so I just pulled my mouth-barbs out, jumped over to his forehead, and sank them into his skin as hard as I could. It was, I imagine, exactly how a jockey got an untamed fathier to behave.

Luke finally understood what I wanted and leapt forward to grab a massive femur bone from one of the rancor's previous victims off the cave floor. Two quick bites on the back of his head later, he turned around and held up the bone like a club.

"Use the Force. . . . Use the Force . . ." I heard him mumble. "Have to use the Force. . . ."

The rancor lumbered forward. One step. Another step.

Luke's legs trembled, and the top of his head quaked like the deck of a ship caught in a solar storm. The boy was scared.

I had no choice but to leap to his ear again. "Let him grab you and move you closer to his mouth. Then stick the bone in his jaws."

He froze for a second before relaxing again. "Oh, like sticking a proton torpedo down the exhaust port of the Death Star," he said. "I understand."

I had no idea what he was talking about, but as long as he obeyed my directions . . . "Sure. Whatever."

I have to give the kid credit. Rash and clumsy as he was, he was brave. As the rancor's claws wrapped around him, he didn't faint with terror or give in to the pain of being squeezed by those crushing, thick fingers. He winced but held on to the thigh bone, and as the rancor lifted him closer and closer to its jaw, he raised the bone and aimed it steady and straight down the gullet of the creature despite waves of hot breath filled with the stench of rotting meat.

"Now!" I shouted, and bit into his forehead before hanging on for dear life.

Luke crammed the bone right into the creature's jaws, lodging the two ends firmly against the roof and floor. Howling with pain, the rancor dropped him. Its yawning jaws were jammed open.

"Go, go, go!" I bit into the right side of his scalp.

Curled up on the ground, Luke was breathing hard and fast. He looked up and saw a small opening to the right, under a jutting ledge. The space was just big enough to fit him. He scrambled into it.

"I used the Force!" he whispered gleefully. Oh, that goofy boy.

The rancor, its primary weapon rendered useless, howled at the grille far above. Jabba cursed in his rumbling, groundquake-like voice; Leia looked like she was ready to faint; and the whole court jeered some more.

Salacious, true to form, summoned some more weak cackles. Without me, he had no idea how to make a joke out of the wacky situation.

But we weren't out of danger yet. With a grunt, the rancor managed to put enough pressure into its jaws to snap the thigh bone like a measly toothpick. The enraged predator then returned to the task of hunting down its surprisingly thorny prey as it lumbered toward the ledge under which Luke was hiding.

Closer and closer the monster came, and then it leaned down to dig Luke out from his hidey-hole. A sharp claw swiped dangerously close to Luke's face.

"Now would be a good time to use force!" I hopped over and screamed into Luke's ear.

"How? How do I use the Force?"

"Not *the* Force, just use some force!" I was so mad that I bit his earlobe, and Luke winced.

The pain seemed to finally get my point across.

Luke grabbed a rock off the cave floor and smashed it down, hard, on the probing claw. The rancor recoiled and reared back, howling in pain.

I looked through the arch formed by the creature's bowed legs. In the far distance, I saw the opening through which it had emerged earlier.

Time for another ride.

I jumped back on top of Luke's head and bit his forehead. "Get up!" I growled.

Thank the Great Mole-Flea that Luke had blind trust in this "Force" controlling him. He scrambled out from his hiding place and ran under the rearing rancor. I picked two spots over his forehead and sank my mouth-barbs into them rhythmically: left, right, left, right. . . . The quicker I alternated my bites, the faster his legs pumped. I doubt any AT-AT pilot could claim to have steered her mount with more precision than I did as I guided Luke toward his destination.

I maneuvered Luke into a full sprint until he ran under the door that had released the rancor and slammed into the control panel at the other end of the dungeon. A small door lifted to reveal . . . an iron lattice that barred the way.

Gaghhh! I cried out in frustration. I thought I had found an escape route, but of course it wouldn't be so easy. Luke grabbed on to the lattice and flopped helplessly like a hooked fish.

"All right," he muttered to himself. "It just *looks* hopeless, but I bet now is the time you show me what to do to take that thing down!"

He was talking to me, the voice of the Force. Even now he wasn't giving up hope. That was pretty touching, actually. He might not be very smart, but he sure was determined and trusting.

All right, I said to myself, *I'm not giving up, either. There has to be another way.*

By then, the rancor had turned around and was stomping back toward its lair, intent on its still-alive dinner.

Jabba's rancor keepers came up to the lattice and jeered at Luke, poking at him with their sticks to force him back into the dungeon.

Luke stumbled back and leaned against the wall, gasping, as the rancor was only a few meters away.

Time slowed down.

A single red light glowed through the gloomy, dank dungeon air from the opposite wall, mocking my plans. I had come so close to saving the foolish boy, to fulfilling my promise to the princess. And all my hard work would come to naught.

I wished I had full control of Luke's muscles. What wouldn't I be able to accomplish if I had that body? I could picture myself leaping onto the back of that lumbering beast and gouging out its eyes, biting into its skin to draw blood. If only . . . if only . . .

The rancor took another step forward and opened its slimy jaws, pawing the air with its menacing claws. . . .

Luke froze.

"I believe in you," he said. "Use the Force."

The universe was not fair. I had such good reflexes; I could lift forty times my body weight. And yet, because we mole-fleas were so diminutive, we were prey for the mantis-crows, and the mantis-crows were prey for the monkey-lizards. The monkey-lizards, in turn, had to avoid annoying the Gamorreans lest they become snacks for the porcine brutes, and the Gamorreans were helpless against the mindless rancors. As each link in the food chain got bigger, it also seemed to become less intelligent.

Wait a minute, I thought. *We just need an even bigger mouth.*

I glanced up at the jagged metal teeth at the bottom

edge of the door that had released the rancor. Each of them was the size of a mountain peak, far bigger than the stalactite teeth of the rancor standing under them.

Time snapped back to its regular flow.

I bit down into Luke's scalp determinedly. Left, left, right, left, right . . .

He stumbled forward and knelt. I jumped to his ear and screamed at him. "Pick it up! Pick it up!"

He picked up the rock in front of him.

"Now throw it!" I commanded him in the voice of the Force.

His arms moved jerkily, and the rock flew out of his hands and crashed into the single red light on the opposite wall. It was the control panel for the gate.

The door slammed down like a giant jaw and instantly crushed the skull of the rancor. With a few final spasms, the humongous body stopped moving.

"I knew it!" Luke said. "I never doubted."

The jeers coming from above quieted. A surprised

gasp from Jabba. Even Salacious had enough presence of mind to figure out that it was not a good time
to cackle. I heard Leia's momentary laugh of delight
before it was choked off.

The rancor's keeper, a burly cliff of a man, stumbled
into the lair and sobbed as he saw the lifeless body of
his charge. I suppose I could understand him. After
all, even I was coming to like that clumsy, stubborn
deluded man-mountain called Luke Skywalker. Whatever his faults, he had an endless supply of hope, and
that was no small thing. He really was growing on me.

Luke slumped against the wall, and I slumped against
his skull, both of us exhausted but delirious with joy.

You might think that the perspicacious thing for
Jabba to do after his pet rancor was killed would be to
investigate what happened and possibly offer a good

contract to the killer—I would have preferred to be directly credited, but I was willing to share some of the credit with my mount. After all, if someone was able to neutralize your fiercest killing machine in such short order, chances are you'd want them working for you.

But instead of the logical thing, Jabba decided that the Wookiee, Captain Solo, and Luke Skywalker—with me still riding on his pate—would all be taken deep into the Dune Sea on his sail barge, where we'd be tossed into the Pit of Carkoon to feed the all-powerful Sarlacc, who would digest us slowly over a thousand years.

Like I said, the bigger they are, the less brains they possess.

There was nothing to do but train Luke for the task ahead. (I wasn't exactly scared, since I could always leap away at the last minute—I did have powerful legs. And even if that didn't work, I decided that if the Sarlacc swallowed Luke and me together, I'd jump in his mouth and make myself a home in his belly. If it took the Sarlacc a thousand years to digest its victims, surely I'd be protected inside Luke and would live out the rest of my life in relative comfort. But I didn't tell Luke that—large creatures rarely appreciate being informed of the ways we small creatures can take advantage of them.)

While we rode through the Dune Sea on a skiff alongside the sail barge, I drilled Luke on a detailed set of hair-pulling commands. It was hard work. The guards had Luke pinned in place, that fool Solo insisted on distracting him with nonsense small talk, and the wind whipped by Luke's ears, making a howling ruckus. I had to cling to the swirly ridge around Luke's left ear canal with all six of my limbs and shout into it to give him instructions on what he was supposed to do based on each distinct pattern of bites. A few times, the wind almost tore me away from him. But I hung on and climbed right back to my piloting perch.

At least I was in the sun. After Jabba's dank palace, bathing in sunlight felt divine.

"The Force is with me," Luke muttered, his innocent eyes wide open as he nodded at my instructions.

By the time we got to the sedentary Sarlacc, it was almost anticlimactic. One surprise: Luke's little astro-mech droid tossed him his laser sword when they finally freed the young man to push him into the monster's mouth. *Does he even know how to use that thing?* I wondered, and I immediately took control.

"Just shut up and do what your tingling scalp tells you," I told him.

He nodded vigorously. "Right. Use the Force. Listen to the Force. I've been through this training."

As deluded as the kid was, he did have good reflexes and strong muscles—for a human. Even though everything was slightly delayed because I had to relay my orders through his scalp, it was no trouble for me to keep Luke alive and defeat his enemies, because every-one was basically moving in slow motion compared with my quick mind.

One hard bite at the very center of his head, and he launched himself straight up, out of the way of the yawning mouth of the Sarlacc; another quick series of nips later, he was tumbling through the air, head-ing straight for the sail barge. *Up-up-down-down* I pulled and pushed my sucking tubes, and *woosh-zing-woosh-zing* went his laser sword, cutting down Jabba's henchmen like giant pasol trees being felled. I pressed my tentacles in deeper and leaned *left-right-left-right*, and Luke swung his laser sword into precisely the right positions to block incoming blaster bolts.

"*Bam!*" I shouted, but it came out as a gurgle, as I had forgotten that my mouth was still firmly embedded in his skin. "*Achoo!*" my mount sneezed. Apparently he was the sort who sneezed when his scalp tingled a certain way. "Good to know," I said after I pulled my regurgitation ducts free. "We'll avoid that in the future. Let's start again!"

Piloting him was overall a pretty amazing experience. I wouldn't say that he was leaping with anywhere near my grace or swinging that sword even one-fortieth as hard as I could have (proportionately speaking), but he was imitating my movements with reasonable accuracy.

I even started making laser-sword humming noises in my head as I drove Luke around. It just felt right.

We landed on the sail barge and wreaked more havoc. I peeked inside and saw Princess Leia wrapping her chain around Jabba's neck and choking him. "Atta-girl!" I shouted. In sympathy I gave Luke's forehead a celebratory bite, and he yelped.

"Sorry!" I shouted. It was fun to see my partner Leia turn the instrument of her enslavement around on that arrogant criminal. I felt Leia and I were spiritual mates, both of us able to impose our will on creatures much larger than we were.

Under my guidance, Luke soon cleared the decks. Monsters spilled from the sail barge as they decided it was preferable to try their luck at fleeing the always-hungry Sarlacc on foot rather than being cut down by the hot fury of the mole-flea-guided spinning Jedi.

Let me amend that. *Smart* monsters jumped ship.

As Luke passed one of the portholes in the barge, I peeked in and was shocked by the sight. There was Salacious Crumb, my former mount, trying to tear out the photoreceptors of that supercilious protocol droid Luke had gifted to Jabba. Instead of leaving the vicinity of the rampaging Luke Skywalker–Lugubrious Mote combo, Salacious had apparently decided that moment was the perfect time to demonstrate his loyalty to His Exalted Blubber—even though Leia had already strangled the gangster boss.

Without me, the monkey-lizard didn't even have a mote of political sense.

"Run! Salacious, run!" I shouted. I knew then just how Jabba's rancor keeper felt.

But he couldn't hear me. Luke's little astromech ran up at that moment to save his gold-plated friend and zapped Salacious with a buzzing electric wand.

Let me tell you, I had never seen Salacious jump that high that fast, or heard him scream in as high-pitched a tone. I laughed and laughed. It was the funniest bit of comedy he had ever performed, albeit he didn't come up with the idea.

With Jabba dead and Leia freed, I had Luke grab Leia, shoot the deck gun at the barge itself, and swing off the barge onto the skiff, where Captain Solo, the Wookiee Chewie, and another one of Luke's friends, Lando Calrissian, had taken control. We took off just as the barge exploded into a fiery ball of flames. I hope Salacious had a chance to get out. He might have been a bubble-headed brute, but he was *my* bubble-headed brute.

I jumped from Luke's head onto Leia's nose.

"You're right," I said. "He did grow on me."

Leia gave me a cross-eyed grin.

I jumped from Luke's head onto Leia's nose.

Despite the loss of my home on Salacious, Leia refused to let me resettle on her.

"Come on," I said, "it will be fun! Two girls together to take on the galaxy!"

She mumbled something about being allergic to furry feet and suggested that I move in on Luke.

"He's a good kid," I said, "and I really do like him. But it will be too exhausting, having to do all his thinking for him."

And I told Leia never to mention me to Luke—the kid was so joyous about having used the Force to save his friends that I didn't have the heart to let him know the truth. I didn't mind not getting credit for the part I'd played; I had given him smarts, but he had given me hope, and I counted myself ahead in that deal.

So Leia found a nice woolly hopwell beast who agreed to take me in as a guest. We traveled around the galaxy for a while before I decided to join the circus. It's a nice life: I get my name on the posters, in bigger font than anyone else's (I insisted on that), and kids love my act.

Leia has done well, of course, but sometimes I think about what happened to Luke. All these stories about him . . . I hope he has learned to think for himself instead of just trusting the voices in his head.

INTERLUDE FIVE

SPLASH. BURBLE. PITTER-PATTER. PLOP.

"Did . . . did you see Lugubrious perform?" G'kolu asked.

Teal chuckled. "Yes. It was quite an act. She had a scaled replica of Jabba's sail barge built—though it was so gaudy it's hard to believe anything like it had ever existed. Inside the barge, the circus installed a fuzzy sandypede larva as a stand-in for Jabba the Hutt. Then Lugubrious leapt and tumbled and dashed about the model with a tiny glowing toothpick that she said was her lightsaber. She made high-pitched lightsaber noises to go with it."

"Wow," said G'kolu. "I wish I could have seen it."

"I think they'd have banned you from the circus after the show," Teal said.

"What's *that* supposed to mean?"

"Let's see. . . ." Teal closed her eyes and concentrated. "You would have stayed behind to debate lightsaber dueling techniques with Lugubrious—"

"Oh, that would be fun! I could get a toothpick and practice with her—"

"That's right. Imagine yourself jumping about the sail barge—"

"And imagine if Captain Tuuma instead of Jabba were on the barge? I'd swing my lightsaber like this—"

"And there, you'd have crushed the stage. Very smooth."

". . ."

"See? I know how you think."

G'kolu tried to change the subject. "Would you . . . would you have wanted Lugubrious to live on you?"

"Um, no. But I can see—"

"Wait!" Flux broke in. "I think we're moving out of the sludge!"

Indeed, the floor under their feet was slanting upward, lifting them out of the odorous slime. They had finally reached the raised platform in the bow of the ship. There, a round access port in the hull would be connected to the sewage pipes to drain the bilge once the *Wayward Current* docked in Canto Bight.

"Wish we had a little light," Teal said. "Hey, what are those glowing things?"

A few maintenance droids zipped through the darkness, emitting a series of staccato clicks as the beams from their searchlights pierced the darkness.

"Maybe we should grab one of those to serve as a lamp," said G'kolu.

G2-X beeped in warning. One of the maintenance droids swept toward the deckhands, and a bright bolt shot out, missing G'kolu's astonished face by mere centimeters.

"*Augh!*" G'kolu jumped back into the sludge from the platform. "Quit it! What's it doing shooting at us?"

"Their programming must have detected us as creatures that needed to be hunted—we're vermin," said Tyra.

The droids hovered in the fetid air, and their humming grew louder as their electric zappers charged up.

"Can't we stop them?" asked Teal. She jumped out of the way as another bolt shot past her, ricocheting off the bulkheads.

"These things are nimble and deadly," said Tyra. "They have to be, because the vermin that live in the bilge can get pretty big."

"Except we're *not* vermin!" said G'kolu.

G2-X beeped excitedly.

"No way. Nuh-uh. Absolutely not," said Tyra.

G2-X beeped some more and whistled sharply for emphasis.

"What's he suggesting?" asked Teal. "I only caught bits and pieces of that."

Tyra sighed. "He says the rest of us need to dive into the sludge to act as bait, and he'll take care of them for us."

"Dive into the sludge? Is he out of—"

Another maintenance droid clicked loudly and swooped for Teal's head. She managed to duck out of the way, barely, but the breeze from the spinning blades passed right over her scalp. She shuddered.

"All right," said Flux, who was preternaturally calm. "It's not a big deal. This slime is made up of the same substance as everything else in the universe."

"You keep on telling yourself that," said Teal. "But the rest of the universe doesn't make my skin crawl."

Flux ignored her. "It's all part of the Tide. We just

need to hold our breaths and dive in. If Luke can jump into the acid mines of the Deep, we can survive being under sewage for a while." She took a few deep breaths, almost gagged, and then resolutely dove into the slimy sludge, burying herself completely.

Tyra, G'kolu, and Teal looked at each other, sighed, and followed suit.

The maintenance droids hovered over the sludge, trying to determine if the targets had drowned or were still active below the surface. Moving silently on his robber wheels, G2-X slowly approached. The lack of body heat emissions from his chassis caused the maintenance droids to ignore him as a threat.

When he judged he was close enough, G2-X burst into a frenzy of motion. He scooped up handfuls of mud from the bottom of the bilge with his manipulators and chucked them into the propellers and exhaust ports of the maintenance droids. As the surprised droids struggled to gain altitude, G2-X leapt onto them like a bird-catching foxcat and pressed them into the thick sludge. The propellers and maneuvering jets sputtered and choked as the droids put up a desperate struggle, but eventually they stopped moving.

The deckhands and the stowaway burst out of the slimy water, sputtering and gasping for air. They gagged and dry-heaved, but eventually they managed to catch their breaths.

G2-X hoisted one of the disabled maintenance droids like some kind of trophy. Its searchlight was still working, and G2-X hung it over the access port like a lamp. The custodian droid chirped proudly.

Teal wiped the mud off her face and spat in disgust. "I'm *never* doing that again."

"I think you made us do that just to see how ridiculous we'd look," said Tyra accusingly.

G2-X let out a noncommittal chirp.

"At least we're safe for now," said Flux. "Who knew that there would be a whole other world down here in the belly of the ship?"

The deckhands had to agree that the adventure was rather exciting.

The companions climbed out of the sludge onto the platform and tried to clean themselves off as best they could.

"We just have to wait until the ship docks and climb out of the sewage pipes," said Teal.

"How long until that happens?" asked Flux.

"A few hours at least," said Teal. "Once the customs inspection is over, the ship has to get into orbit and then glide down to the surface."

"Time enough for one last story?" asked Tyra.

Teal turned to G'kolu. "You're always full of tall tales."

"Make it a Luke Skywalker story," said Tyra. "Stay on theme."

"Well," said G'kolu, "now that you mention it, all

this talk about finding a new world in the belly of the *Wayward Current* does remind me of a story. I once met a scientist from the University of Bar'leth who was possibly the strangest person I've ever known—"

"You didn't look in the mirror this morning, did you?"

"Ha-ha. The scientist wanted to raise money for a research expedition to go inside giant space slugs."

"What?"

"Why would you do that?"

"That's such a strange idea!"

"That's what everyone else said. But her reasons for exploring the space slugs also had something to do with Luke Skywalker. . . ."

THIS IS NO CAVE!

—HAN SOLO

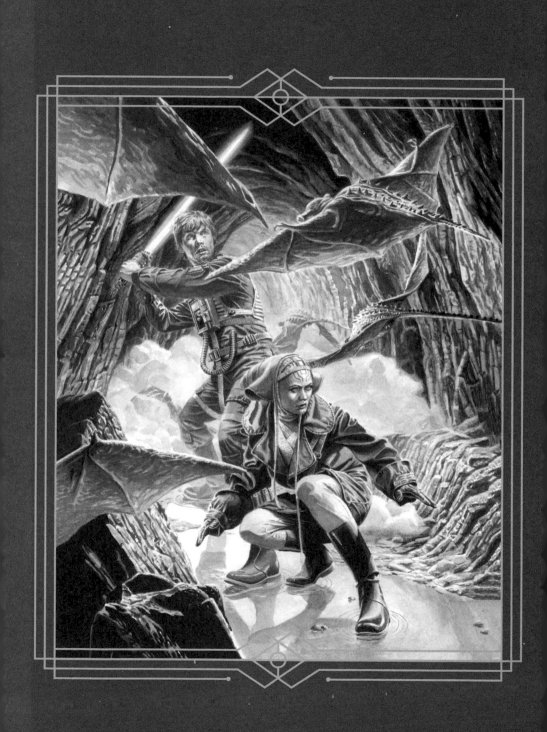

BIG INSIDE

AFTER THREE WEEKS ON A WORLD where the insects had wingspans of three meters and eyes as big as my head, I was very glad to bring out my universal beacon and activate the call for a ride.

I was a young biology student trying to get some fieldwork done in the remote Agoliba-Tu system.

Agoliba-Tu had two life-supporting planets: warm, jungle-covered Agoliba-Ado (where I was) and icy, snowbound Agoliba-Ena (where I needed to go). The orbits of the two planets, with their divergent ecosystems and distinct fauna and flora, were separated by an asteroid belt. There was a debate between my professors over whether Agoliba-Ado or Agoliba-Ena had given birth to life first and colonized the other one, or if life had evolved independently on the two worlds. I was supposed to gather data that could help settle the debate.

Since there were no trade routes through the Agoliba-Tu system, and my university was far too budget constrained to maintain a dedicated research vessel, I had to rely on the kindness of strangers who occasionally jumped out of hyperspace in the system on their way to somewhere else. The universal beacon let anyone popping out of hyperspace know that I was interested in hitching a ride. Watching the flashing beacon and listening to its gentle beeps, I fell asleep.

The noise and turbulence of a spacecraft landing startled me awake.

The ship wasn't something you saw every day: a

two-seat starfighter with an A shape, a worn paint job, and plenty of marks and dents all over the hull. It was probably an old military surplus vehicle that had been converted to civilian use and patched and repaired so many times over the years that it was hard to say if any original components remained.

"Need a ride?" The pilot's boyish, happy eyes twinkled. The lived-in state of the cockpit told me he had been traveling for a long time. "Hop in. I'm Luke."

We chatted as Luke piloted the A-wing through the asteroid belt. He explained that he'd modified the cockpit in part to take on passengers on his long flights around the galaxy as a way to relieve some boredom.

I had a hard time figuring out who Luke was. Some of the things he said made it seem like he had been a fighter in the Rebellion against the Empire, but once he heard that I was an academic, he started peppering me with questions about the worlds I had visited and whether I had seen any signs of ancient ruins of the Jedi.

"Are you an archaeologist or something?" I asked.

He chuckled. "Something like that. I'm trying to learn as much as I can about the Jedi."

Personally, I thought a lot of the legends about the Jedi were either exaggerations or simple tall tales. But many members of the public, who had little knowledge or interest in actual galactic history, seemed obsessed with these legends. Maybe this Luke was some kind of smuggler who specialized in Jedi-related "artifacts." I didn't want to pry. The galaxy was a large place, and it had room for all kinds of eccentric characters.

Regardless of what his real profession was, he was a heck of a pilot. The asteroid belt was packed with obstacles ranging from planetoids as large as cities to rocks barely bigger than my fist. Luke wove and dodged among them as naturally as a fish darting through a coral reef, and he squeezed through some cracks so narrow that I had to close my eyes and pray to every deity I knew in the universe.

"Ha, that's interesting!" he said.

I opened my eyes and saw two bright dots of light flittering and dancing beyond a large asteroid. Their movement reminded me both of the food-signaling dance of Hrelan bees and the mating ritual of Awalian newts. It was so orderly that I couldn't take my eyes away. *Are they alive?*

"Want a closer look?" Luke asked.

I nodded. No biologist would have said no to that.

Luke piloted the A-wing closer. As we approached, the two pinpricks of light suddenly froze, as if aware of our presence, and then zoomed about five hundred meters away, where they began to dance again.

"They're playful!" we both exclaimed, and then we laughed together.

I felt like a kid going after Orowatan fireflies in the backyard. Luke nudged the A-wing to follow the retreating lights, and we began a new dance among the asteroids.

The "fireflies" led us on a merry chase, and Luke swerved and swooped through the dense space debris, nimbly following along. Eventually, the two bright sparks disappeared inside a large cave on an asteroid as big as a moon.

By that time, both of us were eager to track the new creatures to their home. Luke landed the A-wing right outside the mouth of the cave. We sealed our helmets for spacewalking and climbed out of the cockpit.

Gravity on the asteroid was light but sufficient to keep us securely rooted to the surface. Gingerly, we hop-walked to the cave, whose mouth was smoothly polished, as though it had been carved out by a river. I was baffled by the unusual geologic feature. An asteroid that small couldn't have had flowing water.

We stepped into the cave, which was about twenty meters across and about as tall. We turned on our helmet lights and scanned the inside. The walls were covered by long, smooth grooves that again indicated the presence of flowing liquid sometime in the past.

"There!" Luke pointed deeper into the cave, and I saw the flickering lights of the fireflies far in the distance.

We hiked for about twenty minutes as the cave twisted and turned, going deeper and deeper into the interior of the asteroid. My head-up display showed that the temperature was rising steadily (though I still wouldn't call it "warm"). Each time we got close to the lights, they flitted deeper into the cave. Eventually, we arrived at a smooth translucent membrane that barred our way like a frozen waterfall.

Luke reached out to touch the barrier. It gave a little and bounced back, like a rubber sheet.

"This is probably their hive," I said into the helmet microphone, drawing on what little I knew of the biology of near-vacuum ecosystems. "There are some social insects and brinyvores that live in airless environments such as ocean-bottom trenches or shielded moons, subsisting on radiation and other sources of energy. Maybe this barrier is something they've built to protect their home."

I was about to suggest that we turn back—almost any animal would get quite hostile when intruders invaded its home—when Luke held up a hand for me to be quiet. He pressed his helmet's visor up against the barrier and looked through.

"There's writing on the other side," he said, the excitement in his voice palpable.

I pressed my visor up against the barrier, too. The cave continued beyond the membrane and then made a wide turn to the left a few meters in. With the dim light from our helmets, I could just make out letter-like markings on the wall on the other side of the barrier.

Before I could stop him, Luke took out a utility knife and cut a slit through the membrane. He pressed his way inside, and I followed.

Once we were through, the two sides of the slit joined back together and the membrane resealed itself. I pressed my hands against the barrier. The rubber-like sheet seemed to have healed completely, leaving no sign of our surgery.

"I don't understand . . ." Luke's puzzled voice came over the comm.

I turned to find Luke already at the wall examining the writing. I joined him and saw the source of his puzzlement. The markings were regular and resembled writing, but they didn't belong to any script or alphabet I had ever seen.

Up close, I realized that the letters seemed to be carved in relief in the cave wall, and they gave off a faint glow. Luke ran his hands over the letters.

"These . . . look alive," Luke muttered.

I had to agree. The markings pulsed and brightened momentarily as his gloved hands ran over them.

"I wish Threepio were here," he muttered. "He'd know how to read this. All I can make out is 'mist.'"

"Mist?" I asked.

He shook his head, frustrated. "Could be related to the Jedi . . . but I'm just guessing. Looks like someone was here before us. I wonder if this is a warning or an invitation."

It was true that some social insects, though individually not very intelligent, possessed sentience collectively as colonies. But I had never heard of any that communicated by writing inside their hives.

A growing unease filled my heart. "I have a bad feeling about this," I muttered.

As if in response, the floor of the cave lurched and we fell down. A faint glow lit the cave walls in pulsing rings. We felt a bone-rattling rumble that came from somewhere deep down, and the floor and walls shook some more.

"Let's get out of here," Luke said, and he pulled me up. We sliced through the membrane again, and hop-ran for the cave opening.

In the low gravity, our footing was already unstable, but our escape was made even more difficult by the constant jostling and buckling of the ground as the asteroid quakes continued. Like stumbling grasshoppers on Agoliba-Ado, we finally made our way to the last turn in the cave, and I expected to see the stars as we bounced around the last bend. . . .

And we did, except that the oval slice of the heavens was shrinking, like a great eye closing.

"Run!" Luke yelled into his helmet mike. "This must be a cave-in!" We redoubled our pace.

Just then the ground buckled violently again, and I was tossed off my feet and slammed against the cave wall. I tried to get up, but my right leg would not support my weight. I almost blacked out from the pain.

Luke had gone on running about twenty meters before realizing that I wasn't following. Because of the light gravity, it took him several skidding attempts before he could stop and turn around.

"Go on! Go!" I screamed. I could see that the cave opening was now just a narrow slit. "You have to get out!"

"I'm not going to leave you behind," he said, his voice determined. He bounded back, slung my arm over his shoulder, and began to hop-run for the opening again. My right leg hung uselessly, either broken or badly sprained. At least the light gravity made it possible for him to carry me.

But the ground continued to contort and shake violently, which slowed our pace. We watched helplessly as the starry sky narrowed to a slit and then disappeared completely.

By the time we made it to what used to be the cave

opening, we found a solid wall in our faces. Tracing the jagged line in the wall, I realized that the wall seemed to be made from a giant pair of jaws fused together, and we were on the wrong side of the mouth.

All of a sudden, everything made sense.

I slumped to the floor and hung my head between my knees. "We're inside an exogorth," I said.

"Ah . . ." Luke let out a held breath. "A giant space slug. Han would have— Never mind."

I didn't bother correcting him for using the non-technical name. Scientific terminology could wait until we weren't dinner for an asteroid-sized predator.

Luke looked at me. "You're the biologist here, so tell me: are we in danger?"

I shrugged. "Not immediately."

The truth is, even today we don't know a lot about exogorths: giant, silicon-based creatures that live on asteroids and can grow large enough to swallow starships. It's not even clear how many species of these slugs there are, much less what their individual biology is like.

What *is* known is that they tend to live in environments where opportunities to feed are few and far between, and the exogorths have an extremely slow metabolism (they aren't called space slugs for nothing).

"So we could just wait here until it feeds again and escape when it opens its mouth?"

"In theory, yes. But . . ."

I explained that an exogorth rarely moved, and when it did move, it could do so only in quick bursts that exhausted its entire supply of energy. After that exertion to swallow us, it probably wasn't going to move again for years.

"Years?"

"Maybe decades. Probably takes that long to fully digest us."

"This is like being in the belly of a sarlacc," Luke

muttered. He pounded on the rock walls around him.

"If I were you, I'd stop moving around so much. You'll use up your oxygen supply in no time."

"Well, I have no intention of waiting around to be digested."

"We don't have many options," I said. "This thing is basically made from kilometers-thick layers of rocks. I didn't bring any asteroid mining equipment. Did you?"

"I've been in plenty of hopeless situations," he said. "Let's look around. Maybe there's another way out. After all, we know someone has been here before."

I very much doubted that there was another way out, but something in his voice made me think, *Why not?*

We got up and, with him supporting my weight, limped deeper into the beast.

As we slashed our way back through the rubbery film, Luke and I speculated on how our host lived.

"This is clearly a sophisticated predator," I said.

"A *sophisticated* space slug? How?"

I explained that the space slug—it was just easier to use the common term—had probably developed those "fireflies" as lures to attract prey.

"Like an opee sea killer or a deep-sea finned-fry-trap," Luke said, catching on.

"Exactly." I was glad to be talking to someone with a quick mind.

Abruptly, Luke stopped and held up a hand. We were now about a hundred meters beyond the point where we had first seen those letters on the wall.

A piece of wreckage barred our way. It was so old and deformed that it was hard to tell what kind of spacecraft or ground-based vehicle it had once been.

With Luke supporting me and carefully pointing out every foothold, we made our way over the wreck.

Many of the components had dissolved away, leaving behind a mostly metal skeleton. I got the sense that it had been there for centuries, maybe even longer. We didn't see any bodies.

"I think whoever wrote the glowing sign near the entrance came on this," Luke said.

A chill went down my spine. "Why do you say that?"

Luke pointed to a few carved markings on the wreckage. "They're in the same style."

I couldn't really tell, but I trusted that Luke knew what he was talking about. "But . . . if the wreck is here, doesn't that mean they came but never left?"

Instead of answering, Luke pressed ahead determinedly.

The cave around us grew even more sinister in my eyes.

The rubbery film that we had encountered earlier turned out to be only the first of several similar barriers. The barriers got thicker as we went deeper into the exogorth, though all shared the same quality of self-sealing after we went through. We also passed by a few other signs of past victims: the metal remains of a helmet; a piece of some kind of erosion-resistant fabric; a pile of twisted electronic components, long decayed beyond use. I wondered how many others had followed the playful "fireflies" in here over the millennia and never returned.

Luke stopped again and let out a long whistle. Standing next to him, I was also rendered speechless by the sight.

We had emerged into an enormous cavern that was at least fifty meters tall and maybe half a kilometer in length and width. A few meters in from the entrance was the shore of a lake that filled the rest of the cavern.

The beams from our weak helmet lights should never have been enough to illuminate that vast space, and yet I could see the outlines of the distant walls on the other shore of the lake quite distinctly. As my eyes adjusted, I saw that the entire cavern was lit by a faint blue glow that came from the walls. Bright spots of light pulsed in the ceiling, and as they were reflected in the placid surface of the lake, it seemed as if we were floating in space, surrounded by stars.

A loud series of screeches pierced the absolute silence in the cavern, and the bright pulsing lights in the ceiling began to move. They dropped down, gathered into small groups, and headed straight for us.

Luke pushed me into a nook in the wall next to us. He ducked into it right after me and, standing with his back to me, got into a defensive crouch.

A lightsaber came to life in his hands.

In the bright glow of that torch, I saw monsters swooping out of the dark in swarms. Long, triangular wings; elongated heads, half of which were taken up with jaws filled with sharp fangs that glowed bright blue; loud shrieks that merged into one continuous blood-curdling howl.

I shuddered. They reminded me of the bat-like predators that hunted in swarms on the planet Touksingal, where my dissertation advisor had lost an arm to the bloodthirsty creatures. I was sure I was looking at a variety of mynocks that hadn't been studied before.

(The scientific part of my mind realized that the presence of wings meant that the cavern was filled with air. I filed that information away to make use of later, when we weren't under attack.)

Luke stood at the opening of our hideout and spun his lightsaber into a brilliant, impenetrable wheel of deadly beauty. I saw wings, heads, torsos being severed by the humming blade of that weapon, and though it seemed as if thousands of monsters were attacking us, not a single one made it through.

In the glow from the lightsaber, I was surprised to

see no frown of rage or grimace of terror on Luke's face; instead, his features were set in an expression of calm . . . sorrow, as though he was mourning the deaths of the monsters attacking us, as though he was reluctantly doing what had to be done, unswayed by anger, hatred, or fear.

As though they could sense Luke's skill, the monsters suddenly changed tactics. Turning as one, the swarm swerved away from our nook and skimmed over the surface of the lake. Crisscrossing ripples from flying creatures dipping into the water disturbed the tranquil mirror.

What is the purpose of a lake in the middle of an exogorth? My mind churned in search of a solution.

Luke, taking advantage of the temporary relief, deactivated his lightsaber and stood at the opening to the nook, panting and watching our attackers. I crawled up next to him.

"Turn off your helmet light," I whispered urgently.

"What?"

"They're drawn to it!"

He hesitated. Even though the light from our helmets was weak, there was a psychological comfort in its presence that was hard to let go.

"Hurry! We have to move away as soon as you turn off your light. We can't stay here."

"But there's no better cover—"

"We'll die if we stay here!" I slowed down, articulating each word. "You have to trust me."

We locked gazes, and the doubt in his eyes was replaced after a moment by resolution. He nodded and turned off the helmet light. Then he grabbed mine, flicked it on, and tossed it on the ground, right in front of the nook.

"What are you doing?" I hissed. "Give it back!"

"You have to trust *me*."

Ducking down, he indicated that I should get on his

back. I complied without complaining. Then he looked at the sheer cave wall to our right and jumped.

My heart leapt into my throat, but I bit down on my bottom lip to keep from screaming. In the light gravity, his jump took us up about four meters before he grabbed on to a ledge. Then, hand over hand, he shuffled to the right about twenty meters before he found another narrow ledge under his feet, where he set me down. I pushed back from the edge and pressed my back against the cave wall.

The bright swarm, which had skimmed all the way to the other side of the lake, turned around and headed back for the spot where we had been hiding.

I found the wall I was leaning against covered by a layer of slimy mud. I grabbed handfuls of it and began to slather the mud over Luke's suit. After a moment, he understood what I was after and began to slather the mud over mine. Soon we were both completely covered by the slime, which hopefully masked our smells and heat signatures.

Something wriggled in my fist as I dug for another handful of mud. Without thinking, I tossed whatever it was into the lake below. With a gentle hiss, I watched as a white, larva-like creature the size of my forearm writhed in the water, its skin bubbling and dissolving. A few seconds later, it was completely gone.

"Probably strong acid," I whispered into the comm. "Could also be filled with aggressive microorganisms."

The bright glowing swarm had arrived at the nook, still illuminated by my left-behind helmet light. Wave after wave of the winged monsters dove at where Luke had been standing but a moment earlier, and we heard spitting noises and splashes, as though it were raining in the cave.

After a few seconds, the helmet light went out.

Luke pressed his helmet visor against mine. We both nodded, finally understanding each other.

"We're in the stomach of the slug," I whispered.

The monsters had moved away into the lake to fill their mouths and bellies with the deadly corrosive liquid, which they spat out as a kind of venom. If we had remained where we were, no matter how skillfully Luke wielded his weapon, he couldn't possibly have protected both of us from a pouring acid rain. My realization that we were inside the digestive organ of the space slug had prompted me to insist on moving away.

"I didn't want us to be killed," Luke said, "but I also didn't want to keep on killing them." There was a compassionate strength in his voice that felt comforting. "I had to leave a lure in place so they wouldn't keep on looking for us."

Learning from the trick the slug had used against us, he had left my helmet light behind to draw the attention of the mynocks so we could save ourselves—as well as save them.

We drifted across the deadly lake. I gazed by turns up at the pulsing lights on the ceiling—the monsters had gone back to sleep after failing to find us—and down at dim shadows swimming in the depths below.

Our macabre raft was made from the skulls and wings of the mynocks Luke had killed earlier. The hollow skulls provided buoyancy, and the wings, tied together into a large sheet laid on top, made a platform on which we huddled. Since we couldn't be sure that any other material we had with us would withstand the acid in the lake, using the bodies of creatures who lived and hunted with the acid seemed the best choice.

"Who knew there would be a whole other world in here?" said Luke. He was oaring us across the lake, using a paddle made from the bones and wings of the flying monsters.

I said nothing. The stress and excitement from the

attack of the killer mynocks had made me forget the reality of our situation for a moment. But now that the crisis was past, I was feeling despondent. My right leg throbbed. I was trapped in the belly of a monster.

"I'm getting used to the smells," said Luke. "Wonder if we can tell if something is edible by our noses."

Even seemingly good news about our situation could not cheer me up. Since finding out that the inside of the slug's stomach was filled with air and life, Luke and I had cautiously taken off our helmets; it was also an experiment partly driven by desperation, as our suits' air supplies couldn't have lasted much longer. The self-sealing barriers we had passed through evidently acted as airlocks. The air was indeed breathable, though it was filled with strange, fetid smells. It was also quite cold, and I shivered as our breath misted.

"I really wish I knew more about biology," Luke said. "Maybe you could give me some lessons as long as we're in here."

I wanted to scream at him to shut up. His relentless patter was driving me crazy. We were going to die, and he was talking about eating and biology lessons!

"You should stop the raft here, and I'll just roll into the lake," I said. My voice sounded dull, already dead. "Would be quicker to go that way rather than waiting to starve slowly after days of wandering around in this place."

"Sure," Luke's voice was calm, as if my suggestion was perfectly reasonable. "But you should probably strip off your suit first. I'm not sure that the synthetic materials would be healthy for our host. Might give it indigestion."

I was outraged at this suggestion. "I'm sure it wouldn't be bothered by something like that—"

"Why would there be all these creatures living in here?" Luke asked. "They're parasites, aren't they? That can't be healthy. Maybe it's having stomach trouble."

"They're not necessarily 'parasites.' I'm not completely surprised that there's a whole ecosystem in here. *You* have a whole ecosystem of microorganisms living inside you, too, some of them helping you with digestion, others necessary for regulating your body chemistry."

"I have monsters living inside me?"

"If you swallowed something small and foreign, it would probably think so," I said. Luke's questions had triggered the professorial side of me. "The slug has to digest carbon-based prey as well as silicon-based food, and the creatures who live in here probably exist in symbiosis with their host. Over time, they help break down the bodies of prey and intruders into forms that can be more easily absorbed by the host."

"So each of us is as complicated as this slug," he said. "We're entire systems living in balance, not self-contained individuals."

I nodded.

"The universe is full of wonders," he said, his voice full of . . . joy.

I looked around me, and everything appeared in a new light. I was no longer in a hopeless tale of terror but being given a once-in-a-lifetime opportunity. I could probably devote my career to studying the ecosystem in there, an environment no other scientist had explored.

I saw the grin on Luke's face, and suddenly I understood. He had seen the despair in me, and reminding me of what I loved and why I had become a biologist was how he gave me hope again.

"Thank you," I said.

"We're going to get out of here," he said. "Just learn as much as you can while you're still inside. I certainly want to learn all I can about those glowing letters—" He pointed to the wall we were approaching.

I was squinting to make out what he was pointing at when something massive bumped at us from below, hard. Everything exploded into chaos: Luke and I rolled off the raft; a massive tentacle broke through the surface and slammed down, breaking the raft apart; a bright glow lit the length of the tentacle looming over us like a spacecraft from some unknown world; the pulsing lights of the flying monsters hanging on the ceiling scattered, screeching all the while.

The cold solvent chilled me instantly, and then, a second later, a burning sensation covered every inch of my face. I closed my eyes and mouth, but I had already swallowed some of the deadly liquid, and I could feel my throat burn as I struggled to suppress the desire to scream and swallow more. The burning liquid seeped into my cuffs and collar, and pain like I had never felt before burned my hands and neck, traveling up my arms and down my chest.

I wasn't going to make it out after all.

A powerful arm grabbed me around my waist and pushed me through the icy lake.

I blacked out.

⟨✦⟩

"You'll be all right. . . . We're past the stomach now. . . ."

Luke's visage floated in and out of focus. His face was full of scars, and the deadly digestive juices of the space slug had eaten away his beard. Our suits had offered some protection for the rest of our bodies, but the exposed parts were burned. He looked haggard, worn, but still unbowed.

"Water . . ." I croaked. But the pain was so overwhelming that my feverish brain shut down again.

When I regained consciousness, I felt something sweet and refreshing being poured into my mouth. I forced my parched tongue to separate from the roof of my mouth and swallowed the life-giving water gratefully.

After I finally stopped drinking, Luke fed me bite-size pieces of something soft and cream-colored. It tasted like roasted flesh. I felt strength returning to my limbs. Even my right leg, which was tied to a splint, seemed to throb less.

"What . . . what am I eating?" I asked.

"You don't want to know," Luke said, chuckling. "There are fungi growing in the gut of the space slug, along with small creatures that I've never even seen pictures of. I tried to eat small pieces of each and see how my body reacted. There were a few that made me sick, but this is safe."

"And the water? How did you get the water?"

"I was once a moisture farmer," he said. "I can get water out of anything."

Somehow his smile and upbeat tone, despite the

fact that we were both injured, made me feel as though being trapped inside a space slug wasn't the worst thing in the world.

"I guess we keep on going?" I asked. "I want to see what's in this thing's gut before I die."

"Of course," Luke said. "And I'm going to find out who wrote those glowing messages. Oh, and we're not going to die. I *don't* have a bad feeling about this."

Time inside the exogorth didn't work the same way it did outside. Without a spinning planet under our feet or automatically synced chronos on a spaceship, our circadian rhythms soon went awry. We slept when we were tired, ate when we were hungry, drank when we were thirsty, and explored every path open to us. I had no idea how many days we spent inside the slug, whose interior offered a whole universe to explore.

Perpetually feverish, racked with pain and discomfort, and facing danger at every turn, Luke and I nonetheless managed to map out practically every square meter of space that we could reach. The exogorth was a maze of tunnels and interconnecting chambers. Some of the chambers were mired in perpetual darkness, while others were lit with various kinds of luminescence, biologically generated and otherwise.

The glowing signs appeared several more times. Sometimes they consisted of writing that Luke pored over for hours, trying to decipher its mystery. Other times they were paintings, abstract curlicues and starbursts and crosshatching woven together to present awe-inspiring scenes that took up a whole wall. We gazed at them as though looking at the swirling, churning galaxy itself. These tapestries of light were both map and territory.

"Whoever they were, they were fantastic artists," said Luke.

I had to agree. But I was admiring a great artist myself: the laws of nature that made the exogorth
possible.

The chambers presented a variety of climates and
fauna and flora, as though they were individual worlds
connected by hyperspace jumps. We passed through
mist-filled chambers populated by silicon animal-
plants that seemed to ooze as well as walk; we crawled
through wet, almost tropical tunnels that were densely
carpeted by mosslike fungi that tasted of spices and
gave us lurid dreams; we trudged through swampy caverns where giant serpentlike creatures peeked out of
the muck from time to time, gazing at us with glowing
eyes on top of stalks.

"Nobody is going to believe any of this," I said. "No
one ever thought to look inside an exogorth for life."

"Nobody believed me when I set out to recover the
knowledge of the Jedi, either," said Luke.

"Aren't the Jedi mostly a myth?" I asked.

"As much as new worlds waiting inside space slugs," he said.

"But magic isn't the same as science."

He laughed at that. "Real magic is always knowledge. The galaxy is knowable, and that's what makes it wondrous."

Time after time, we fell into traps or monsters came after us. Whether the creatures we encountered were parasites or simply semi-independent organs of the space slug, Luke always managed to get us out of those scrapes. The space slug must have been so sick of the stomachache we were giving it as we continuously defied its attempts to kill and digest us.

I took copious notes and drew sketches. Luke and I discussed my biological theories and speculations about all the mini-ecosystems we encountered along the way. We also talked about the luminous writing and drawings, and Luke explained to me that he thought they were related to the Jedi religion. The gathering of knowledge in the face of our certain doom kept us sane and gave us the drive to go on, step after step, fight after fight.

Then one day we took a new turn and emerged in a chamber we had not been to before.

The semispherical cavern was covered by a soft carpet of grasslike vegetation, and the entire roof glowed with a pearlescent luster that made it brighter than all the other places we had been to. An altar-like structure constructed from neatly stacked rocks dominated the far wall. Despite all the wonders we had already seen, that chamber took our breaths away.

"I think . . . this was built by *them*," Luke said. He did not need to explain who he meant.

We approached the altar and saw a group of life-size sculptures on top. There were three of them: one human and two from an insectoid species. All three were dressed in flowing robes, and the carving of the folds in the clothing was so intricate that they seemed to be flapping in a breeze.

"No sign of erosion," Luke said. "It's as if they were carved yesterday. I can't even imagine how this was possible."

The three figures stood in a circle and were all looking up at the glowing ceiling of the dome. Though I couldn't read the insectoid expressions, the woman's face was in a state of calm rapture, as though praying. There was more glowing writing near the feet of the figures, though we still couldn't read it except for the symbol that Luke thought meant "mist."

"Beauty is a language of its own," Luke said. He sat down before the altar, leaned back, and admired the statues. I sat down next to him and did the same.

"They probably made these before they died," I said. "This was their last defiant gesture to the universe, to proclaim that they were here."

"That's not a bad last message."

A sense of peace came over us. The weariness from days of hiking through the maze inside the space slug, always having to stay vigilant, lifted. Somehow, I could tell that we would be safe there. It was a spiritual place, a refuge.

We fell asleep.

"Wake up! Wake up!"

I woke up, still confused and groggy. Luke was shaking my shoulders and pointing at the statues. I looked, and then all drowsiness left me as my heart pounded wildly.

The three statues had moved while we were asleep, and they were looking down at us. The compound eyes of the two insectoids appeared like honeycombs while the woman's gaze was placid and warm, the light of life shining in those silicate eyes. She was leaning toward us, her hands outstretched.

"I . . . don't understand," I said.

Luke took a few steps closer to the statues.

"Don't!" I shouted. Visions of how we had come to be inside the space slug haunted me. What if it was another trap? What if we were simply seeing what we most wanted to see? Wasn't hope also the greatest lure and bait?

But Luke's face looked rapturous. "It's safe. I can hear them."

"*Hear* them? What are you talking about?"

He waved at me to be quiet and walked all the way up to the altar. He bowed to the three figures and then raised his supplicating hands to the woman, grasping her stone fingers.

Luke shuddered as though struck by lightning.

I ran over and tried to pull him off but couldn't. His body grew stiff as his movements slowed. He seemed to have become a part of the statue as life drained out of him. I screamed in despair.

Then he let go and fell back onto the ground, gasping. I rushed up to him and cradled his limp figure in my lap. Sweat drenched his face, and he looked as exhausted as if he had been physically exerting himself. But there was a look of pure wonder on his face.

"I heard them. I heard them."

It has been a long time. . . .

Once, the galaxy was a different place. The stars were younger and closer to each other, and some of the spinning globes around them were still raw, unformed. But the wanderlust was just as strong and the sense of wonder as insatiable.

The three of us, Shareen, Awglk, and Wkk'e, were master weavers of the Luminous Mist. Our art was to knot and entwine the strings of Mist that cradled all the sentient species and connected the far-flung worlds to one another to create glowing portraits of the Mist's all-encompassing magnificence. The Mist connects all of us and grows from all of us; it endows birdsong and cwilikdance with joy; it uplifts the downtrodden with laughter; it comforts the left behind when their loved ones fuse into the Mist-Beyond; it's the bright essence that pulses within each cell of our being, far more important than the superficiality of our rough material shells.

We traveled around the galaxy seeking out new wonders to be depicted on our loom, to give the ineffable form and color.

One day, we landed in a belt of stones strung out in space like a trail of crumbs in a dark forest. The sense of foreboding was palpable.

Bright sparks flashed among the stones and danced away. Excitement. Thrills. Adventure.

I know, a Mist-Weaver is not supposed to crave these things.

But the heart wants what the heart wants. We followed the sparks.

Into the trap we fell, like ships tumbling down a gravity well. We were sealed inside the belly of the beast. No crumb trails led to the way out. In circles we turned, twisting, winding, gyrating, like a shuttle caught in an endless back-and-forth that led to no new pattern, no advancement, no way through.

We sat down, ready to die.

Wkk'e was the one who would not give up. It was the nature of members of her species to pass from the larval stage to the adult stage by enclosing themselves inside cocoons in which the children slept and dreamed the Long Dream.

"What if we built cocoons for ourselves out of the Luminous Mist?" she asked.

So we wove our masterpiece, the most beautiful weaving in the history of Mist-Weavers. We spun the formless form of the Luminous Mist into resilient silk strands that contained the hidden dimensions of the universe; we twisted them into yarn that was strong enough to bind time; we wove them into a sheath that we wrapped around ourselves to slow time to a crawl—a shroud and a birth caul at once.

Inside this cocoon, the three of us waited. We stretched one lifetime into thousands. While an eon passed in the grand universe, but a second had ticked by within. We waited as the beast that swallowed us grew. We waited as more adventurers came after us and died after their brief sojourns. We waited as we forgot what else to do, content to let time devour us, even as we sought to stop its passage.

Once in a while, when visitors came, we pulled aside

a few strands in the cocoon and let a bit of time slip in. We liked to watch the strangers.

"This one is unusual," said Wkk'e.

"Yes, I sense it, too," said Awglk. "I've never seen such a bright Mist Heart. It's more brilliant than a thousand suns."

We admired the Bright-Heart for a while, and then I noticed something else.

"I sense a rot in the Mist," I said. It had been millennia since we last gazed outside the cocoon into the grand, Mist-filled universe. "There are . . . so many holes in the Mist. A darkness has come and corrupted it."

The pain of watching our beloved Mist so debased was wrenching.

"Bright-Heart means to restore the beauty of the Mist," I said.

"How do you know this?" asked Wkk'e.

"Bright-Heart wants what all bright hearts want," I said.

"But he's trapped here, just as we are," said Awglk.

Trapped. I thought we had found a way to escape death, but we had only been lured by the fear of death into imprisoning ourselves in stasis. I hadn't realized how much I missed the turbulent flow of time, the violent palpitations of hope. Until Bright-Heart had come.

"We must offer him our help," I said.

And I explained how.

Wkk'e and Awglk were silent for a while.

Awglk asked, "Are you sure?"

"No," I said. "I'm not sure. Were we sure of the future on the day we fell in? None of us can ever be sure of the future. But we can hope. And without hope, we'll never know."

Wkk'e and Awglk responded in the way I knew they would, from the Book of Luminous Mist: "Hope is the knowing heart of Eternity."

"Time flows incredibly slowly for them. Even as they sped up the flow with a small slit in their cocoon, it took them all the days we've been trapped in the exogorth to have that short conversation."

Luke tried to explain the Mist-Weavers' offer to me. He spoke of how much we still didn't understand about the Force, of ancient wisdom and lost arts; he described the way time could be converted into energy and vice versa; he drew pictures with a stick in the mossy ground to show me how cocoons could be unwound in an instant to unleash eons of pent-up time, like a massive flood held back by a dam until released with an explosion.

I didn't understand most of it, to be honest. All I knew was that the Mist-Weavers had figured out a way to save us.

"You mean there's a way out?" I exclaimed. "That's wonderful!"

"They can't unwind the cocoons themselves," Luke

said. His voice trembled, and I sensed that something terrible and momentous was being unveiled to me, even if I didn't understand the full import of his words. "I have to cut the cocoons open with my lightsaber."

"Then let's do it!" I said. The heat of hope filled my chest, drowning out the vague sense of dread.

"You don't understand," Luke said. "They'll die."

His words pounded against my heart, as heavy as stones. I stumbled back. "Oh." I tried to find something more appropriate to say, but my mind was blank, overwhelmed by the revelation.

I looked at Luke and took stock of our situation. There were lesions on our faces, and our wounds had never fully healed. The food we were eating inside the exogorth was deficient in certain nutrients and not fully compatible with our metabolism. Though we had tried to keep a positive attitude, our bodies were slowly, inexorably failing. The cocoon of decay was tightening around us, and I knew that we were growing weaker and sicker with each passing day. We weren't going to last much longer.

Luke's eyes were locked on to the statues. He sat there, unmoving, as though he had turned to stone himself.

It was one thing to sacrifice yourself for something you believed in, but how much heavier was the burden of accepting someone else's sacrifice?

I watched Luke's face go through a range of emotions: sorrow, regret, terror, anger.

I watched him pace around the chamber and remonstrate with the statues, pleading for another way.

I watched him sinking to the ground in despair, cradling his head between his hands.

He muttered to himself, and I caught only fragments of sentences.

"I've seen too many sacrifices. . . . Obi-Wan . . . If only Master Yoda could have taught . . . I can't . . . useless . . ."

I left him alone with his thoughts and went away to collect food and water. I couldn't stand to watch him struggle with an unbearable weight, and I didn't know how to help him.

When I returned, I saw that Luke was again holding hands with the statue of the woman. His body was shaking violently.

Alarmed, I ran up to help him, but he let go and stumbled back. I caught him and held him up.

"I once watched a dear friend, who was also my teacher, face the very embodiment of evil in a duel," he whispered.

I listened, knowing that no response was required.

"He knew that he couldn't overcome his opponent by force, and yet he needed to save me and our friends. So when he saw that I was near the ship that would take us to safety, he stopped fighting and allowed his opponent to cut him down. But in fact, he had released himself from this world and become part of the Force. What the enemy had cut down was only an empty cloak."

I could only imagine what an awe-inspiring scene was summarized by those simple words.

"Surprised, the enemy focused all his attention on the discarded cloak, forgetting about me and my friends. That was my teacher's intent: to use himself as a lure to distract the monster. We escaped, and I have never been able to forget the look my teacher gave me before he died."

Luke's voice was growing stronger. He had emerged from the wrenching struggle within his heart.

"It was a look of pure peace and contentment. No fear, no anger, no regret, no sorrow. He became stronger than his enemy could possibly imagine because he knew it was time to let go. He trusted the Force. It was a lesson I still have a hard time accepting. . . ."

He pointed at the statues. "Do you see her face? That's the exact same expression my friend and teacher had before he faded into the Force."

Luke turned on his lightsaber and gently plunged it into the opening between the three statues. Sizzling arcs of energy connected the lightsaber with Luke and with the Mist-Weavers.

There was no fear in his eyes, or regret, or anger. Only a deep, abiding reverence.

The statues glowed brighter and brighter. I could feel the heat emanating from them. I pulled back instinctively and tried to pull Luke after me.

"No," he said. "It's all right. Let go of your fears." His voice was suffused with utter faith and trust.

He gestured that I should pull down the visor of my helmet, and I did so.

The statues appeared to be made of molten iron. They were so bright and gave off so much heat that I had to shield my face. And still they glowed even brighter.

With a quick, agile side step, Luke slashed the lightsaber down, as though cutting through a sheath shimmering between the glowing figures.

Turning off his lightsaber, he stepped back and bowed deeply to the statues before pulling down his visor.

I risked peeking through the cracks between my fingers. The statues were coming to life, as though they were melting wax figures. The woman embraced her companions, and I could not tell if her expression was one of sorrow or joy.

Then her face settled into a tranquil smile, and I saw nothing in her eyes but resolution.

Now, she seemed to say.

Luke spread his arms to shelter me.

And the world disappeared around me with the light of a thousand newborn stars.

There was a new, gigantic crater in the side of the asteroid. We lay on its rim, gasping in our suits, like two fish that had been tossed onto the beach by the tide.

Later, after we stumbled back to the safety of the A-wing and Luke took off his helmet, I saw wet streaks on his face.

"There are patterns in the Force, like the rise and fall of the tide," he said. Maybe he was talking to himself; maybe he was talking to me. "Deeds from the past echo in the present. The Mist-Weavers were lured here eons ago by bright sparks; we were lured here by the same lights. My teacher once acted as a lure to save me; we saved ourselves from the flock of monsters with another lure. My teacher freed himself from fear and doubt to save me; the Mist-Weavers freed themselves from fear and stasis to save us. I once watched as my teacher died, feeling helpless; only now do I understand that accepting the sacrifice of those who love us and share our ideals is the first step to becoming more powerful than we can possibly imagine."

It was, in truth, a speech too mystical for me to fully grasp. I was never well versed in the tenets of the ancient religion of the Force.

But I thought back to the way Luke had kept the flames of hope in me alive; the way he had protected me and rescued me, even when it put him in harm's way; the way he had made sure that I didn't stop admiring the wonders around me. He was my friend, and I was grateful that his sacrifices had freed me from the trap of despair and the lure of dejection to love the galaxy more.

I understood enough.

"I'm sorry all your notes were destroyed during the escape," Luke said.

We were on an ice-covered lake on Agoliba-Ena, where I was determined to complete the study.

"There will be other chances," I said. "I'm thinking of switching to exogorths as my specialty."

"You haven't had enough of being inside one?"

"It will take a long time to digest everything I've seen, and who knows what wonders are hidden inside others?"

"There is always more knowledge to seek in the galaxy," he said, a grin of understanding on his face.

I nodded and stepped back.

The A-wing took off, leaving behind a melted, slushy trail on the lake. I watched it disappear into the sky, knowing that I would have to face an uphill battle for the rest of my life to get people to believe what I had seen. The inside of the space slug was big—really, really big, like the universe hidden inside each of us, like the eternity curled inside each second.

The galaxy is knowable, and that's what makes it wondrous.

But it didn't matter. It was enough to have glimpsed what no one else had seen. It was enough to have witnessed the Mist that suffused the universe parting for one second to reveal the bright heart of wonder and hope underneath.

DREAMS AND HEROES

THE FATHIERS MOANED from time to time in their slumber. Who knew what kind of dreams they dreamed?

The *Wayward Current* glided out of the sky over Canto Bight like a drifting leaf and touched down gently among the glittering pleasure domes connected by necklaces of arched walkways. Nestled at the feet of towering mountains next to the shore, the city was like a bejeweled empress seated on her throne, dipping her toes into the sea.

Armies of heavy stevedore droids swung into motion, connecting air hoses, supply chutes, cargo conveyer belts, and water and sewage pipes.

The sluices at the stern of the ship opened, and torrents of fresh, clean water poured into the bilge, dissolving and diluting the filthy sludge as garbage and grease slicks floated on the rising surface. At the other end of the ship, the bow, the round access port whirled open, and the grimy tide, filled with dead vegicus, space barnacles that couldn't hold on to the hull, yearling bilge-water lobsters, and three young deckhands, a stowaway, and a custodian droid, spilled out of the ship into a wide sewage pipe.

"Hold on."

"Grab my hand!"

"Don't let go!"

"DWEEP dweep!"

"I've got you! I'm not going to let go!"

"I know."

They tumbled out of the pipe into a massive pool the size of a small lake. There, the sewage would settle and be filtered, and the water recycled for more dockside uses. Pulling, kicking, and keeping one another afloat, the band of adventurers splashed their way to the edge of the pool and climbed ashore.

Even the authorities there didn't think the sewage reclaiming pool was worth guarding.

"Welcome to Canto Bight," said G'kolu to the others with a dramatic flourish. The dunk in the pool had washed off the grime of their time in the bilge, though it would take some time for their clothes to dry.

They looked around in delight. Massive domes loomed above and around them, each grander than the last. Lit from within by bright lights in every hue of the rainbow, they appeared as a fluther of jellyfish rising into the still indigo predawn sky. Ships zoomed through the air in every direction. Loud music and advertisements filled their ears while the smells of a thousand perfumes and exotic foods assaulted their noses (and horns). In the distance, waves of noise from cheering crowds swelled and receded like an invisible ocean.

"Must be the fathier racetracks," said G'kolu.

"So this is the galaxy," said Flux, a smile of wonder on her face. She turned to the others. "Thank you for helping me see more of it."

"Do you think Luke Skywalker is here?" asked an eager G'kolu. "Is that why you came here?"

Flux closed her eyes and seemed to reach out into the cacophonous air around her. The others held their breaths and gazed at her intently.

She opened her eyes and shook her head.

"Oh." Teal was disappointed.

"I told you there's no such thing as the Tide," said Tyra.

"That's not it," said Flux. "Luke isn't here. But the idea of Luke brought us together. That's how the Tide works. Aren't you glad we got to meet? From now on, no matter how far apart we are from each other, we'll be connected by this shared experience, by this night. This is our story, and it's the best story of them all."

"We're all Luke Skywalker," said G'kolu, his horns standing straight up jauntily.

"We uplift each other," said Tyra.

"We have to head back before Tuuma throws a fit when we aren't there to unload," said Teal.

G2-X beeped at Flux, and she used her robe to wipe away a bit of mud that seemed to be stuck over his photoreceptor.

"Be well," said Teal. She and Flux embraced each other.

"Trust in the Tide," said Flux.

"May the Force be with you," said Teal.

Flux turned and walked away from the lake, her plain white robe dazzling in the bright multihued lights of the metropolis. Soon her figure faded into the busy traffic.

"Let's go," said Teal. She kept her voice low, hoping the others would not hear it crack or see the tears in her eyes.

At the loading dock, the deckhands ran into Dwoogan and Ulina.

"I didn't see you at breakfast," said Dwoogan. "Were those vegicus tails from last night too rich?"

"Not at all," said G'kolu. "We were up early and wanted to check out the casinos before unloading."

"Really?" said Ulina, her eye patch glowing a suspicious orange. "I was in the cargo bay before we docked, and I never saw any of you leave."

"We were . . . um . . ." Tyra and Teal looked at each other desperately.

"We snuck out in the captain's skiff when he left to see the dockmaster," said G'kolu. "You know how he would never let us ride it, so we just jumped on the back once he settled in. It's not like he can turn around easily with that body, you know?"

Dwoogan guffawed with delight. "You're really bold."

"They don't call me 'the Grease' for nothing. I'm slick."

"You know the captain hates—" Ulina started to lecture.

"You gonna tell me that you never tried anything like that when you were a deckhand?"

Ulina sighed and shook her head, her eye patch glowing an affectionate, tender aquamarine. "Go take care of the fathiers and get them ready to be unloaded."

"Yes, ma'am!"

"I left some extra food for you in the galley," added Dwoogan.

"If you finish ahead of schedule," said Ulina, "I'll let you start your shore leave early this afternoon."

The deckhands whooped with joy.

"What about the two of you? What are you going to do in Canto Bight?" asked Teal.

"Bet on a few races," said Dwoogan.

"Look up some old friends and swap some stories," said Ulina.

"Oh, we already have some great stories," said Tyra.

"I'll bet," said Ulina. "Just by the way G'kolu's horns are twitching, I know you've been up to no good."

"Hey!"

While the organics continued their banter, the droid custodian G2-X wheeled himself away. He had been away from a power source for longer than was his habit, and he was feeling the effects of his night of exertion.

As the conversation behind him faded, G2-X turned the corner and found a power socket. He plugged himself in and drifted into low-power mode. He was looking forward to dreaming about electronic fathiers and juice bars filled with the purest power chargers.

Briefly, just before his cognitive circuits went into free association, he wondered what the deckhands would dream of when they slept. He hoped that their dreams would be filled with adventure in a galaxy more wondrous and beautiful than the wildest tales could conjure.

He was certain they would be the heroes of those adventures, each of them a Luke Skywalker.